ALL EXPENSES PAID

ALSO BY ZOE ROSI

Courier

Pretty Evil

Someone's Watching Me

ZOE ROSI

LIGHTHOUSE
—— BOOKS ——

Text copyright ©2025 by Zoe Rosi

Cover design ©2025 Cong Nguyen

Published by Lighthouse Books, United Kingdom

ISBN: 978-1-7384976-6-9

CHAPTER ONE

Influencer Saffron Clark poses in a Chanel scarf, leather jacket, and jeans, with a Louis Vuitton Neverfull dangling from her arm, looking radiant and flawless on Oxford Street. Her post has 22,000 likes and 234 comments.

'Stunning, babe!'
'So gorgeous.'
'Lovelovelove the bag'
'You are just the coolest girl!!'

Debbie rolls her eyes and keeps scrolling.

Another influencer, with 1.2 million followers, reclines on a hotel bed, professionally made up and wearing a jewelled gown that looks like Oscar de la Renta. She's tagged the TV awards party she's heading to. Seventy-four thousand likes. Hundreds of adoring comments.

Even a girl Debbie met a few years ago at a PR party for an injectables brand, who only has ten thousand or so followers, smiles in the dappled light of a winding path in Santorini.

And what is Debbie doing?

Debbie is sitting in a nail salon in Brentwood, Essex, having a pedicure.

Her manicurist slicks on layers of red, her head bowed. Debbie notes her childish hairband, embellished with sparkly doves.

Debbie's had her nails done by the same woman maybe a dozen times, or two dozen, but they've never really spoken. The language barrier doesn't permit it—or at least that's what Debbie tells herself. Their conversation is limited to Debbie pointing at the shade she wants and her manicurist telling her what a 'great choice' it is.

As her manicurist paints on another coat, delicately at the edges, Debbie wonders what her life is like. Where she lives. If it's a nice place. How much she gets paid. If she's happy. But then Debbie wonders why she's wondering that, and the thought evaporates, dissipating as quickly as it came, and Debbie looks back down at her phone.

She spots a post from Jenna Ray, who started her Instagram page at around the same time as Debbie and, like Debbie, has a blonde, blue-eyed pin-up kind of look. Jenna is on a yacht. A huge yacht on the Amalfi coast. She's sunbathing on the deck in an Eres bikini, skin bronzed, hair tumbling over her shoulders, toasting the camera with an exotic cocktail the same shade as the sea.

Debbie clicks through the pictures Jenna has posted from the yacht, wincing a little more as each shot reveals greater and greater heights of luxury.

Debbie doesn't notice at first when her manicurist—whose name is Daisy, not that Debbie has asked—checks to see if she's happy with her now-finished manicure.

'Miss? Debbie?'

Debbie looks up this time. She notes her manicurist's expectant face and glances down at her feet, taking in the ruby-red polish, shining under the bright lights. Her feet, freshly moisturised and lightly massaged, look dewy and pretty.

'Great, thanks,' Debbie says.

Her nails look nice, but she's not exactly thrilled.

Jenna's on a yacht.

A fucking yacht.

Debbie has never been on a yacht, not once, and the jealousy is real. Really fucking real. Real and raw, right in her chest.

Why is Jenna getting to go on yachts and not her?

Debbie's sexy. Debbie's cute.

In fact, Debbie thinks, as she puts on her Gucci sliders and heads to the counter, she probably has a nicer figure than Jenna.

Actually, she knows she does. Her legs are longer. Her waist is thinner. Her breasts are shapelier. And her hair is thicker, glossier. For fuck's sake.

So why Jenna and not her?

Debbie swipes her card over the reader. Daisy is all polite smiles, all 'please' and 'thank you,' but Debbie just wants to leave.

She steps out onto the overcast street—lined with SUVs, cutesy boutiques, and mums pushing prams. Stifling suburban boredom under a cloudy October sky.

Debbie examines her freshly painted nails, fingernails matching her toes. They're perfect, as always, shimmering in the light.

Briefly, Debbie considers some kind of Instagram post. And then hates herself for it.

Everyone and their mother gets a fucking manicure. It's fucking basic. It's not even worth a story.

Debbie needs to share something interesting. Something extra. Something exclusive. Something *enviable*.

Something like a yacht trip.

Sighing, Debbie heads back to her car.

CHAPTER TWO

Luxe Americana is the restaurant of the moment. *Everyone's* posting about it.

It's very Instagrammable, with classic American diner décor. Retro but high-end, like something from a movie set. It opened in Chigwell a few months ago, and it's on everyone's pages.

It will have closed down in a few years, when it's been visited by nearly every influencer in Essex, as well as others from London, and everyone posted about it, and it's no longer new and interesting. Business will tail off. A few regular people will come along—families who don't understand that this is a restaurant where you go to pose, not to eat; teenagers who think the place is cool; and couples looking for a romantic date.

But by this point, the owners—restaurateurs Sally and Martin Jenkins—will already be shutting up shop, having made over £1m from the place. This isn't the first time they've taken on an old restaurant, gone all out with Insta-worthy décor, hired a top social media manager paid infinitely more than the chef, and gained free press from Sally's university friends—contacts from her Oxford days, who now occupy journalism positions at nationals.

Sally will end the lease, fire the staff, shut down shop, and take a three-month break in the Bahamas with Mark—a reward for all their hard work—where they'll both read novels and sunbathe and snorkel and plan their next hustle. Sally will wonder about writing that novel she's always dreamt of while knowing deep down that she probably won't.

Debbie isn't really interested in going to Luxe Americana. It looks nice and all, and she really ought to go—it is the restaurant to be seen at right now—and yet, it feels sort of lame to be posting the same stuff as everyone else. Debbie wants to be different. She wants to be extra. But she knows it's good for engagement to join in with what other people are talking about. Her friend Amelia booked a table for them both weeks ago, securing a coveted slot in the restaurant's extremely busy bookings diary.

Debbie's still rankled by Jenna's yacht trip, and she's not really in the mood to go out. She hasn't posted anything for a while now, though. Her last post was a paid one posted last Thursday, in which she waxed lyrical for ten minutes about an eyeliner she hadn't even used. She needs more content, relatable content. And maybe getting dressed up and seeing Amelia will be fun. It might lift her mood.

Debbie attempts to compensate for the lack of originality of the venue with a striking outfit, hoping it might make her posts stand out. She goes for an ironic, sexy trailer trash look: cutoff shorts that show off her lean thighs, a cropped graphic tee under an Yves Saint Laurent denim jacket, hi-tops, and an imitation Burberry cap—a dupe so good no one could

10

possibly tell from her Instagram pictures. No point buying the real thing, Debbie reasons. Half her 'designer' stuff is fake. It's not like her followers can see the dodgy seams or feel the cheap fabric.

Debbie likes what she sees in the mirror. She looks good. Playful. And as she strikes poses, admiring her reflection, her mood does indeed start to lift. She takes selfies and posts stories, and the likes and messages that pour in send so much dopamine firing through her brain that by the time she arrives at Luxe Americana, her mood is positively buoyant.

Debbie crosses the restaurant and notices other girls eyeing her, sizing her up, as well as designated photographer boyfriends looking her way. Debbie smiles to herself.

Amelia is sitting alone, waiting. She sips from a glass of sparkling water. Debbie has known Amelia since school. They weren't really friends until sixth form, when Amelia took Debbie under her wing, deciding that for whatever reason she was worthy of 'popular crowd' status. Before that, Debbie had been a bit of a nobody. Not exactly an outcast, but not cool. She was bookish, a swot who flew under the radar. But with Amelia's endorsement, she started being invited to parties; she started getting attention from boys.

She and Amelia never really hung out one-on-one, though, and when school ended, they went their separate ways, not bothering to keep in touch aside from the odd comment or like on Facebook. But when it transpired that they were both doing Instagram and both living back in Brentwood, they got in contact and started spending more time together. Nearly every time they've met up, it's been at a PR party or an Insta-worthy location, and they've taken pictures. A lot of pictures. Debbie isn't really sure if they're friends or just working together to boost each other's pages.

Amelia had been all over the local press when they first re-connected. She'd been caring for her grandmother, who had dementia. She uprooted her life in London, where she'd been working in events, to move into her grandmother's two up, two down. Amelia tended to her grandmother's needs so she wouldn't have to go into a care home and leave her beloved house, the one she'd lived in her whole life. She started her Instagram page to have something that was 'all hers,' 'a little escape,' 'a place to connect with people her own age during an isolating and overwhelming time,' as she told the press. Her page blew up, gaining over 100,000 followers in a few months, and attracting attention from brands. The local papers presented her as a sexy Mother Teresa. Brentwood's caring Kardashian. Gorgeous and cool but with a heart of gold.

Amelia's grandmother has since passed away, and these days Amelia spends her time at press parties and posing in designer clothes in enviable locations, but she still carries a halo from those days. Debbie wishes she could have someone to care for or something meaningful to set her apart. She started her page because she was hot and vain and wondered if she could get freebies.

Debbie appraises Amelia's outfit. She, too, has defied the typical nice-dress-and-fancy-nails combo with her trademark goth-lite look. She's wearing a black velvet dress, heavy eye makeup, and a crucifix, her jet-black hair worn down. Amelia isn't a goth at all. Her favourite film is Little Miss Sunshine; she jogs around the park every day at 6am, and she has a 'good vibes only' affirmation as her phone screensaver, but she looks *really* good in black, and she knows it. Her pale alabaster skin and long dark hair is very Morticia Adams, and cranking up the goth look for the gram gets her all the likes.

'Hey babe,' Debbie says.

'Hey!'

The girls lightly embrace.

'You look amazing,' Amelia says.

'Thanks, babe. So do you. Love your dress.'

Debbie clocks the new Cartier Love Bracelet on Amelia's wrist, which doesn't really go with her outfit but which she obviously wanted to show off nonetheless.

'Ohh, nice.'

Amelia tells her about the shopping trip she took to London a few weeks ago, a Selfridges haul with her mum and dad—'so much fun, we went *all* out'—followed by dinner at The Wolseley. Amelia's father is a property developer whose portfolio took off a few years ago when he bought some decrepit office blocks, did them up, and let them out to a high-paying insurance firm expanding from London. Now he has more money than he knows what to do with. The family has moved from their modest semi to a seven-bedroom house set within its own private grounds. Amelia's father, Michael, bought her a flat too, not far from the family home.

Debbie listens to Amelia recount this lovely day out with a polite smile and polite comments, even though she feels pissed. Debbie hasn't spoken to her own father for years. He disappeared when she was nine and never looked back. Amelia knows that. And yet she still goes on about her lovely, generous dad, without a care in the world. Debbie reminds herself that her issues are her problem. Amelia is just sharing her life. She should be a supportive friend. But she can't help feeling jealous. She can't help feeling sad.

'Oh look, Holly's here,' Debbie comments, clocking well-known local influencer Holly Nightingale, who got famous after featuring on a popular reality dating show, going from a modest ten thousand followers to well over a million. She just got engaged to an Arsenal striker, and she features regularly on the Daily Mail site. Debbie wonders briefly if paps will be outside the restaurant tonight. If she could get snapped somehow.

'Seriously?' Amelia looks over her shoulder.

Holly is with a gorgeous redhead Debbie doesn't recognise. Maybe another influencer. They both look stunning.

Amelia turns back.

'Is she still engaged to that footballer?'

'Yeah, think so.'

'Wow. Knew this place was worth coming to.'

Debbie looks at her menu.

'So what are you having?'

'Think I'm going to just get something classic. Burger with all the trimmings. Onion rings or something. You know, since we're here.'

'Yeah, I think I'll do the same.'

Debbie's stomach rumbles, and a part of her wishes she could just order a huge burger, sit somewhere totally private, alone, with no one watching, and devour the whole thing. Every last fry. Every last mouthful of meat. Every last slither of cheese and gherkin. But it's just a daydream. Debbie eats no more than 1,500 calories a day. Most days, it's more like 1,200. To consume anything more would be an indulgence she would never allow herself.

A waiter comes over and takes their orders.

Double cheeseburgers. Sides of curly fries, coleslaw, onion rings.

Debbie orders a porn star martini. Amelia, a mojito.

The waiter, Jake, a drama student, thanks them and heads back to the kitchen. From one look at them, he already suspects most of their food is going to end up in the bin or vomited into a toilet bowl. He keeps telling himself he should quit this job. Some days, it really drags him down to see so much waste. It makes him think of his childhood, how his mother scrimped and saved, shopping at Asda, getting the reduced stuff. And yet all these rich girls order food just to take photos. But as far as jobs go, there are worse. Jake knows that. The customers, despite being annoying, tend to tip. The hours aren't too long. The bosses are alright, and, well, the girls are pretty.

While Debbie and Amelia wait for their food, they catch up. Amelia's on-off boyfriend, currently off—Sam—who she's been dating since school, has apparently been sending flirty messages to some girl Amelia can't stand. She misses him, but they haven't spoken for a while. She ran into his cousin the other day at the gym, who mentioned that he talks about her 'all the time,' so she's pretty sure there's still something between them.

Debbie tries to concentrate and make all the right noises, but she's bored. She's heard variations of this stuff over and over again. Sam and Amelia have been on and off for years, circling around each other, drifting in and out of each other's lives. They'll probably end up married at some point, with kids. And they both know it. They just do this stupid dance with all these meaningless dramas.

The waiter brings over the cocktails, and Debbie is grateful for the distraction.

Photo time!

Debbie gets a compact mirror from her bag and checks her reflection. Amelia does the same. Then, wordlessly, they swap their phones across the table and start taking pictures.

They smile into the camera, trying to look sexy, but also relatable and cute, and confident and cool, and not too try-hard, while working their angles. Always working their angles. Snap after snap after snap. Diligent, wordless, methodical. It can take a hundred shots sometimes to get one that's exactly right. But after a couple of dozen, both Debbie and Amelia are happy, studying their phones, zooming in and out, making mental notes of Photoshop tweaks to do later, occasionally taking sips of their cocktails.

Their food arrives, and they swap phones and go through the routine again, posing and pretending to bite into their burgers.

Snap, snap, snap. They take their phones back and inspect the pictures, redoing some of them. Their food is going cold, not that it matters. They didn't come here with eating in mind. Debbie's had one bite of her burger at this point and two fries. Amelia's had the same.

Debbie finds she isn't satisfied with the appearance of her nose in some of the shots. It's shiny. So, sighing, she dabs it with powder, and Amelia retakes her pictures.

Debbie inspects them, satisfied now. She looks hot. The pictures should do well.

The girls pose together for a story, laughing at nothing, having *the time of their lives*. They tag the restaurant. Then they take snaps of their food and their cocktails, and they joke around in each other's stories, speaking into their phones to update hundreds of strangers, their over-exuberant smiles falling away the moment they stop recording.

In total, Debbie eats five fries and has four bites of her burger. It's not actually that nice. Not only is it now cold, but the meat is chewy and bad quality, some factory-made patty. The burger bread is a bit stale, the cheese flavourless. It's not surprising to Debbie. She's been to dozens of these restaurants, places that have gorgeous décor that looks pretty on the grid and highly questionable food. In a way, the inedibility of the food comes as somewhat of a relief—it makes resisting eating so much easier.

Amelia pulls her burger out of the bun and starts cutting into it like it's a steak.

'Need the protein,' she comments as Debbie watches.

Their phones are down; this will not be documented.

With a lull in conversation, Amelia brings up Debbie's love life. Or lack thereof.

'Seeing anyone?'

Debbie scoffs. 'No!'

Debbie finds she doesn't know what to make of men these days. She used to have romantic fantasies of marriage and kids and happily ever after, but after the hundredth, or maybe two hundredth, DM from a man hitting on her, whose feed is shamelessly full of pictures of his 'missus,' his home life, and even his kids, she's sort of lost faith in the whole thing.

Does romance actually exist, or is it a bit of a sham? Can you really trust men? What if the ones who seem nice are just better at faking it than the others?

The thought of ending up in a relationship with a man who'd DM a young woman, calling her 'gorgeous' or complimenting her 'tits,' before cosying up to his other half makes Debbie want to be single forever. To be with no one but her chihuahua, Angel.

And yet deep mistrust of men bordering on pure misandry isn't really a socially acceptable or dinner-friendly stance, so Debbie tells Amelia that she's 'still looking'.

For a while, Debbie would screenshot the messages she was getting from these men. She'd save them to a folder on her phone entitled 'Fucking Assholes'. She had vague intentions of exposing the men in this folder, sending the screenshots to their wives and girlfriends, until the sheer quantity of offenders became so overwhelming that she lost her motivation. But she still adds pictures to her album, an odd compulsion, creating her own personal evidence file.

With the love life topic waning, Debbie recalls a DM she received from a brand selling tops that change colour while worn—'wearable mood rings'—wanting to collaborate, and asks Amelia if she got it too, which it turned out she did. And then the girls discuss business until the waiter comes along to ask if they've finished eating. He collects their plates, his instinct right. More food destined for the bin.

'Dessert?' Debbie suggests, contemplating a few ironic retro shots with an over-the-top sundae, perhaps. She pictures herself, sucking suggestively on a cherry. Her followers might like that.

Amelia squirms.

'I don't know. I think that might be a bit too much.'

Too much food or too much content?

'We don't want to look like we're obsessed with this place, you know?'

'Yeah, you're right.'

So the girls pay and get up to leave.

They don't bother tipping Jake, and he smiles tightly, sighing to himself as they walk away.

CHAPTER THREE

Debbie's post from last night, featuring three snaps from Luxe Americana, posted at 10.30pm, after she had time to do a few Photoshop tweaks, currently has 3,343 likes and sixty-three comments.

'The most beautiful!'

'Wow! Unreal!'

'So hot.'

'Your outfit is amazing!!'

'Looking even more delicious than the food!'

Amelia's picture, heavily edited to the point that she looks cartoonish, in Debbie's opinion, has 7,777 likes and 92 comments.

'For fuck's sake,' Debbie grumbles as her little dog, Angel, snuggles up to her.

Debbie tickles Angel's soft fur, breathing in its familiar and comforting smell. Angel licks her face.

Debbie reminds herself that Amelia does have more followers. She does post more. She has been doing this for a bit longer. And it's not like her own post isn't doing well. It's got 22 more likes already, and yet, she still feels behind. She still feels down.

Tickling Angel with one hand, Debbie keeps scrolling. She flicks through stories and then spots one from Luxe Americana.

They've shared Amelia's post and written, 'Thanks so much, Amelia, for coming to Luxe last night! We're so glad you had a great time!'

Stomach squirming, Debbie checks all their stories. Perhaps her post was shared too, and she missed the notification. But no. They've shared a dozen influencer posts from girls at the restaurant, personally thanking each of them for coming along, but they haven't shared hers. Has she been snubbed? She wants to be thanked by the restaurant too. Other influencers saw her there. Not being included is embarrassing. And the restaurant has hundreds of thousands of followers, Debbie could do with the exposure.

Debbie checks the tag on her post, making sure it's correct. It is.

So how did they miss it?

Did they see her picture and decide it wasn't good enough? Debbie zooms in on her nose. Definitely not shiny. She looks fine.

Is she not influential enough? She has 129,000 followers. That's decent.

'Fuck!' Debbie groans.

She jumps off the bed, crosses the room, and looks at herself in the mirror. She's pretty, obviously. So what's their problem?

She sucks in her stomach and presses her hand against it. She stands to the side and examines her profile. She looks slim and shapely. She pulls her scrunchie from her hair and lets it fall around her shoulders, running her hand through the waves. She's always had thick, luscious hair, 'pony hair' her mother used to call it. Without a doubt, her best feature.

She checks her post again. She looks like she's having fun. She looks sexy and cool. It's a good post.

Debbie thinks of Jenna in her yacht. Holly with her lavish life and her footballer boyfriend. She thinks of Amelia, with her alabaster skin and all her hundreds of thousands of followers and endless adoration and likes, and she flops onto the bed, slumping as Angel paws at her back.

CHAPTER FOUR

Debbie pounds the treadmill in her garage gym, pausing to look at her phone every five minutes.

It's been two hours since she noticed the snub from Luxe Americana.

Her post now has 4,074 likes, 98 comments, and 18 shares.

She's lost track of how many Amelia's post has. She hasn't looked for a while.

Debbie checks Luxe Americana's page again, thinking that maybe their social media manager missed her post but has now shared it. She's liked a few of the restaurant's pictures in the past hour or so, in an attempt to nudge them, but no. There's nothing. They've shared every other influencer's post but hers. Great.

Debbie places her phone back down and pounds the treadmill some more. Fuck it.

Feeling reckless, she heads to the kitchen and decides to comfort eat three carrots and half a pot of hummus. Around 300 calories, just under a quarter of her daily allowance. Debbie sinks into the sofa and turns on the TV, watching *Killer in My Neighbourhood*.

She tries to get into the storyline of a woman slain in bed, a brutal murder that horrified the residents of her parochial village, but it's not really going in.

Debbie checks her phone. A DM.

Hi Debbie,

I hope this message finds you well. My name is Yusef Farouqi, and I am the manager of luxury hotel Mirage Royale.

I've been browsing your page, and I'm extremely impressed by your content and audience engagement. I believe your style, personality, and the tone of your page align well with the customer base we strive to reach at Mirage, and I wondered if you might be interested in discussing some lucrative promotional opportunities?

Debbie rolls her eyes. No doubt a time waster. And she's not in the mood.

She's about to block when she has an idea. She types a message.

Interesting proposition. Venmo me £2k, then we can chat.

She includes her Venmo details and smirks.

Nothing for a moment, then a message.

Done.

Ellipses as he types.

I like your style.

Debbie laughs, assuming this guy's bullshitting, but then a notification comes through.

Yusef Farouqi paid you £2000 for a chat.

No way.

Debbie opens her Venmo account, and there it is. Two thousand pounds.

She clicks back into her Instagram DMs and types a message.

Okay, I'm listening...

CHAPTER FIVE

It turns out that Mirage Royale really is a big deal. It has 364,000 followers. It's twenty-five storeys tall, palatial, with sprawling penthouse suites featuring jaw-dropping panoramic views, a Michelin star restaurant—two in fact—a luxurious spa with salt caves, caviar treatments, an oxygen bar, a spectacular rooftop pool, and even its own mall.

It's extraordinary, and Debbie can't quite believe the conversation she's having with Yusef. He's offering to fly her first class to stay there for a five-night all-inclusive trip. It's not that the place doesn't host influencers regularly. As Debbie scrolls down the hotel's page, she spots at least a dozen girls she recognises snapped there, as well as a few celebrities too. But Debbie didn't quite realise she was at this level.

Yusef insists however, that Debbie's visit will help the hotel gain 'exposure'. He mentions that he wants the hotel to 'appeal to the right people', people like Debbie and her followers.

Debbie's flattered. She can't help it.

She spots a picture of Yusef Farouqi himself standing in front of the hotel, dressed in a pristine robe and wearing a big, charming smile like something from a toothpaste ad. He looks wealthy, distinguished, sophisticated. He looks nice.

Debbie starts to feel excited, the sting of Luxe Americana's snub fading. This hotel makes that place look embarrassing. Cringe. *This* is the kind of place she wants to be posting about. *This* is more like it.

So what sort of content will you need from me? Debbie messages.

Yusef starts typing.

He sends a list of content requirements. Ten pictures, in various locations around the hotel. Nothing too difficult, and it hardly seems to warrant a free holiday, but perhaps this kind of thing is normal, Debbie wonders. She knows of other influencers who get invited on free trips all the time. Maybe she's finally levelled up. Maybe she's finally getting the recognition she deserves. Debbie replies.

Okay, that sounds fine.

Yusef requests Debbie's email, and within minutes, his assistant, Samara, has sent a contract formally listing her content obligations, as well as a non-disclosure agreement. Debbie's never received an NDA before for any brand work, and it strikes her as a little odd, but she reasons that maybe this is a cultural thing. Or maybe this is what big hotels do. She's only really worked with make-up and fashion brands before; perhaps the tourism industry does things differently.

Yusef messages.

Once you've had a look over everything, let me know if you wish to proceed, and I'll get Samara to book your room and flights.

Debbie laughs, shaking her head.

She wants to type, 'Seriously?' but she also wants to play it cool. Act like being invited on an all-expenses-paid trip on the other side of the world is the kind of thing that happens to her all the time.

Sounds great, she messages.

This feels so surreal. One minute, she's watching TV, doing nothing, down on her luck, and now she's being offered a luxury trip. Social media really is wild.

Debbie can already picture herself by the pool, sunbathing on a lounger, sipping cocktails. She can already imagine the likes, comments, and attention.

Feeling pumped, she has an idea. Maybe Amelia could come too.

She sends Yusef a message.

Could I bring a friend? She's also an influencer.

Debbie links to Amelia's page, knowing her pictures and follower count will likely impress Yusef.

He doesn't reply.

Not for seven whole minutes.

Angel licks Debbie's face. Debbie tickles her neck. Still nothing from Yusef.

Debbie tries to concentrate on the TV.

She starts to feel uneasy. Has she pushed her luck?

Was it not enough that she was being offered an all-expenses-paid trip? Did she go too far by asking to bring a friend?

What if Yusef loses interest now? Ghosts her?

Debbie reasons that at least she made £2,000 from the conversation, which isn't bad for a ten-minute chat. It would be annoying not to get to stay at Mirage Royale, though.

Or maybe Yusef is just checking out Amelia's page.

Debbie waits another five minutes, flicking listlessly through TV channels, barely taking anything in.

Then finally, her phone buzzes. It's him!

Yes, your friend Amelia is welcome to come and stay at the hotel with you. We can send her the contract to ensure she is happy with the requirements.

Debbie smiles, impressed. The whole thing does sound legit, despite having arrived so out of the blue. The hotel definitely takes an unconventional approach, but it's clearly efficient.

The money in Debbie's account already makes her feel valued, appreciated. None of the brands she's worked with in the past have paid her just to discuss an opportunity, but maybe they should. It's certainly got her attention.

Thank you. I'll talk to Amelia and get back to you asap, Debbie types.

Yusef replies.

Great, speak to you soon.

Debbie hops off the sofa. Angel looks at her expectantly.

'I'm going on holiday, honey!' Debbie tells Angel, as she calls Amelia.

Amelia answers on the third ring.

'Hey,' she says, sounding bored.

Excitedly, Debbie explains the proposition.

'So, some random man wants us to come and stay at his hotel?' Amelia clarifies.

'I know it sounds crazy, but he sent me £2,000 just for talking to him. Look at their page. It's such a nice hotel!'

'It sounds really crazy, actually.' Amelia sighs, and Debbie keeps talking, enthusing about the hotel's rooftop bar, mall, spa, and everything else.

'It does look quite nice. Who did you say had been there?'

Debbie reels off a list of influencers and gives Amelia a moment to check out their posts.

Amelia goes quiet for a moment.

'Sophia Jones went there?' she says, and Debbie can sense Amelia's interest is piqued.

Debbie recalls one of the pictures the Notting Hill-based influencer posted from her trip to Mirage Royale—a shot of her dining at the hotel's fusion Michelin restaurant, a rainbow of sushi spread before her.

'Yeah, and Aster Hicks,' Debbie adds, remembering another influencer Amelia likes who recently visited the hotel, posting a zillion shots by the rooftop pool.

'Come on, it's legit.'

'Alright,' Amelia relents. 'I guess it does look okay.'

'Bloody hell, Amelia. You were more excited by last night's burger!'

Amelia laughs.

'Okay, fair enough. I'm excited! It looks cool!'

'That's more like it.'

And then Debbie and Amelia start discussing dates.

CHAPTER SIX

The next day, Debbie and Amelia sign their contracts and commit to their trip at Mirage Royale.

Soon after, Yusef's assistant Samara emails over their hotel booking and flight tickets.

Debbie is still half-expecting the whole thing to be a wind-up. It feels too good to be true. She even double-checks the plane tickets are real by calling the airline and verifying the details.

But everything is confirmed. She really is going!

Debbie doesn't hear about it, but in her flat in Chigwell, Amelia is also carrying out checks. She gets in touch with the airline too and finds as many posts as she can find from other influencers about Mirage Royale, trying to assure herself that this really is just a very lucky and exciting opportunity. She wants it to be. She hasn't been invited on many trips, and the hotel does look nice. Really nice, in fact. And yet, something feels off. *If something seems too good to be true, then it usually is*, she thinks, reminded of the motto her dad used to drum into her. And yet, Amelia has signed the contract. She's committed herself. She's going.

She wonders if maybe this knot in her stomach is simply unease about going so far away. Amelia has never really enjoyed travelling. She knows she should. You're meant to, right? When you're young and carefree. And yet, she doesn't really like being away from home.

She likes her home comforts. Her cosy bed, with its nice blankets and pillows that are just the right firmness, her kitchen with its familiar foods, the Starbucks down the road. She likes her routine. She likes hanging out in Essex, venturing to London here and there. Sometimes she goes for day trips, to Southend or to visit National Trust castles with her parents—a bit sad maybe, but those places make great backdrops for content.

And Amelia can just about tolerate Spain, at a stretch. She's been going since she was a child. Her family always rents a flat in the same block in Alicante. People speak English in the shops, and you can even buy Heinz ketchup and Walkers crisps. It feels sort of like a home away from home. But this trip? To a country she's never been to, never even considered going to… She's not sure. She sits in front of her laptop, picking at her cuticles—an anxious habit—and she fears she's going too far this time, literally.

How did she let Debbie talk her into this? Debbie normally takes the lead from her, not the other way around. She's been trying to help Debbie grow her account for years, and yet after an initial boom in her first year, Debbie's following seems to have stagnated at around the 130,000 mark. Amelia keeps telling Debbie to keep things consistent. And yet, although most of Debbie's pictures are fun, sexy, and carefree, occasionally she posts these weird, long, rambling captions, musings about life that just don't work.

Amelia sighs. Perhaps she felt sorry for Debbie. She's been so excited about this trip. So thrilled to be asked. Amelia doesn't want to go, but she can't quite bring herself to let Debbie down.

And anyway, it will be good for content. That's undeniable. Shots at the lavish hotel, shopping at high-end boutiques, quad biking in the desert—her followers will eat it up. She just needs to get over this nervousness. Push through this barrier. Once she does, then maybe she'll end up having a really good time. Maybe she'll surprise herself, even get a taste for adventure. Maybe.

Amelia scrolls through the pictures of other influencers having the time of their lives, and she tells herself she just needs to relax, be brave, optimistic. She tells herself it will be fine. It will all be fine.

CHAPTER SEVEN

Debbie prepares for her trip.

She gets her nails done again. This time going for something a bit extra. Gold polish that twinkles like a glitter ball.

She gets a fresh tan, too. Spends hundreds of pounds on outfits—thanks, Yusef. She doesn't exactly need new clothes, but she needs to look perfect, and so she reasons that the discounted broderie Zimmerman dress and incredibly realistic Prada dupe sandals are definitely worth buying.

Debbie has outfits planned for every day and every activity: lying by the pool, sightseeing, clubs, bars, quad biking, even business meetings and hookups. You never know.

She and Amelia start planning an itinerary, packing as many exciting things into their five-day trip as possible. Neither is particularly keen on the tandem skydive they book—Amelia has had a fear of heights for as long as she can remember, and Debbie would rather sunbathe, but the pictures will be worth it.

Both girls tease their followers with trip prep, sharing snaps of bulging suitcases, talking about outfits, and asking for travel tips even though they already know exactly where they're going and what they're going to do.

Debbie's engagement shoots up. Her followers are as excited about the getaway as she is.

She starts to wonder what she'll do next. Where things will go from here. Will she be invited on more all-expenses-paid trips? Could this be the start of something? Perhaps she could lean into the travel niche. She daydreams about herself in Paris, posing playfully under the Eiffel Tower. Maybe visiting Santorini, like everyone seems to these days.

Debbie packs her outfits carefully, placing each outfit in its own plastic zip bag. Debbie considers labelling them—'dinner outfit casual' or 'dinner outfit dressy' etcetera—but she's worried Amelia will take the piss, so she just packs one suitcase with night outfits and one suitcase with day outfits and hopes she'll remember which outfit is for which activity. Debbie fills a third suitcase entirely with shoes.

Rifling through her much-neglected swimwear drawer, Debbie packs five bikinis and three swimsuits for the pool and then changes her mind and packs ten bikinis. She owns dozens. Far more than a young woman living in Brentwood could ever actually need, but half of them were gifted. She thinks of all the content she can get by the pool. All the brands she can plug. And all the new followers she's going to get from this trip.

Debbie messages Amelia, who, it turns out, has packed a dozen bikinis.

The girls message constantly. Discussing places they'll go, sharing ideas for pictures, and talking about brand deals ahead of the trip.

Amelia has scored sponsorship with an upcoming Shoreditch sunglasses label, whose shades she's agreed to wear in all her outdoor content during the getaway. And she's agreed to make a reel by the pool promoting a sunscreen brand, who are paying her £2,500 for a three-minute video.

Unnerved by Amelia's efficiency, Debbie reaches out to a couple of brand contacts. She gets one out-of-office reply. A marketing manager from a fashion brand she worked with about six months ago says they'll look into it and get back to her, but the message feels like a brush-off. A couple of other enquiries go unanswered. Debbie contemplates packing the juicer she's been on a retainer to promote for the past year, thanks to a marketing assistant who seems to have taken a shine to her, and then she realises that would be ridiculous. Who takes a juicer on holiday?

Having finished packing, Debbie starts watching endless reels and videos about the hotel and the area. She can't get enough. She seeks content beyond Instagram too, checking out travel blogs, Pinterest, and TripAdvisor. She even ends up reading Google reviews.

Out of curiosity, Debbie clicks onto Mirage Royale's lowest ratingss.

Breakfast was not enough and not that nice. The air con broke and it took two days for the staff to fix it. Not recommended for a relaxing stay.

Another.

The room smelt smelly like cheap air freshener. Receptionists were loud and unhelpful. Bad grasp of English.

Debbie yawns. And then there's one that catches her eye.

This review will probably be gone in 24 hours. They keep getting them removed, but that's not going to stop me from creating new accounts and posting.

If you are a young woman, DO NOT GO TO MIRAGE ROYALE. DO NOT ACCEPT AN INVITE FROM THIS PLACE.

I cannot stress this enough. YOU WILL REGRET IT. Trust me. PLEASE don't go there.

Debbie scoffs. She clicks on the reviewer's profile. No profile picture. No name, just a bunch of digits. One review.

For a moment, Debbie wonders if she should screenshot the review and send it to Amelia for a laugh but then decides against it.

She's not sure Amelia would find it funny. And deep down, with an anxious twinge at the pit of her stomach, she's not really sure she finds it funny either.

Forcing it out of her mind, Debbie snuggles in bed with Angel. She watches trashy horror films on Amazon Prime until she falls asleep.

The next day, she sees the tab on her phone with the Google reviews of Mirage Royale. The creepy negative review is gone, and weirdly, Debbie feels a chill.

CHAPTER EIGHT

Debbie braces herself to drop Angel off at her mother's place.

Gillian, Debbie's mother, has agreed to look after the dog for the five days Debbie will be away.

Debbie's chest is tight, her breathing short and shallow as she drives through the Brentwood streets, with Angel on the passenger seat beside her in her carrier. Her head aches, and she rubs her temples while pausing at the traffic lights. She reminds herself to breathe. Just breathe.

She draws in a deep breath as the lights turn green.

Debbie has to psych herself up every time she visits her mother. There'll always be a dig, an attack, a look, a put-down, which will trouble her for days, making her feel hurt, annoyed, indignant. Debbie's mother somehow always manages to make her feel like she's not good enough. Debbie knows her mother is jealous and competitive, narcissistic, damaged. But that doesn't take away the pain, the hurt of it all.

She dresses down whenever she sees her, doesn't wear make-up, tries to look unattractive.

She never brags, never talks about successes, brand deals, or romantic interests. She avoids anything good, or anything that might make her sound too pleased with herself, just in case it puts her mum's back up.

She never talks about failures either. Because any struggle, any issue, any mistake will be weaponised against her, filed away for future use, as evidence of Debbie's intrinsic inadequacy.

So Debbie cannot share, good or bad. She has to be neutral and understated. She has to tread carefully.

Sometimes she contemplates cutting her mother off. If anyone else treated her the way her mother does, she'd cut them off in a heartbeat. But it's her mother. And if she cuts off her mum, she'll have no one.

It doesn't help that her dad isn't in the picture. He used to promise to visit when she was a kid. After he moved out of the family home, he sent presents at birthdays and Christmas for a while, until Debbie was around thirteen. He said he'd come and visit, 'once he got settled'. Yet the process of getting settled seemed to take years. Years and years. And then the birthday presents stopped, the Christmas presents stopped, and he went quiet. He stopped having any involvement with Debbie whatsoever aside from fulfilling his legal obligations to pay child maintenance.

He's online. He smiles out from an 'about the team' page on his company website, and Debbie used to send him emails now and again. She wanted answers. She wanted to know why he'd stopped speaking to her, acknowledging her. She was angry. She wanted to tell him what she thought of him. She wanted to let him know how much he'd hurt her. She thought if she could just find the right combination of words, then he'd realise, he'd understand, he'd show some compassion, some remorse, some love. But her emails always and unequivocally went unanswered.

Debbie was an irrelevance, of no consequence. She was someone you moved on from, forgot about.

Debbie's had counselling over the years. She's been heard. She's received compassion. She's been assured that her father's and her mother's behaviour isn't a reflection of her worth, etcetera, etcetera. And she knows in logical terms that it isn't. But that doesn't take away the pain and the loss. No amount of counselling can soothe the disappointment and rejection Debbie feels, deep down.

As Debbie reaches her mother's street, she goes over safe topics she can talk about with her: the weather (chilly lately) or the new shopping centre opening at the end of the road. Or just her mother. What she's been up to. What she's been watching on TV. If she's read any good books lately.

Debbie parks at the end of her drive.

'Come on, Angel,' she says chirpily, trying to ignore her quickening heartrate as she lifts Angel's carrier out of the car and takes her bag of things: food, toys, and a blanket.

She heads to her mother's front door and presses the bell.

Debbie's mother opens the door.

'Oh, hello,' Gillian says, her expression blank. She's wearing a ratty jumper, and Debbie notes she looks tired and old.

Debbie feels something close to sympathy, care, but the feeling is blunted, suppressed.

Gillian opens the door, and Debbie carries Angel in. She tries not to let the lack of a smile, the lack of warmth, get to her.

'So, how are you?' Debbie asks.

'Fine. I was just watching Strictly,' Gillian says.

'Okay.'

Debbie looks down at the carrier.

'Do you want to come out, Angel?' She asks, leaning down.

Sometimes Debbie wonders if she and her mother would see each other at all if it weren't for Angel. Despite her mother's flaws, she's good to the dog, and Angel loves her. Ninety percent of her and her mother's communication these days revolves around Angel, with Gillian looking after her whenever Debbie goes to London or embarks on trips. Gillian isn't the sort of person who'd go out and get her own dog, but somehow Angel has burrowed her way into her heart.

'What are you doing on this trip?' Gillian queries.

'I'm promoting a hotel.'

Her mother scoffs.

'Are you being paid?'

'I'm getting a free trip.'

'So that's a no. Who's organising this?'

'A top hotel.'

'Right.'

Debbie opens the carrier door, and Angel pads out. Angel sniffs her mother's feet and wags her tail enthusiastically. She paws Gillian's legs, gazing up at her with big loving eyes.

'You know, your cousin, Lauren, just got a promotion. She's a partner now at her firm! Partner at twenty-eight years old. Incredible. And she's engaged.'

'I know, Mum. You told me.'

'And you're gallivanting on free trips to strange hotels, honestly.' Gillian shakes her head.

Angel continues pawing at Gillian's legs.

Sighing, Gillian reaches down and picks Angel up.

'I'm young, Mum. I have a right to enjoy my life.'

Gillian rolls her eyes while tickling Angel's neck.

'And yet, I'll be the one picking up the bill.'

Debbie looks away. Despite all her followers and the brand deals she gets here and there, Debbie's broke. She's got more bags and shoes and dresses than she can count, and yet she's maxed out three credit cards, and she's deep into her overdraft. She's a fraud, and only her mother knows it. She flexes online like she's wealthy, but on three occasions this year, she's had to call Gillian, begging for a loan to pay the rent of her one-bedroom flat. And she hasn't paid her back.

'I'm trying to build my following so I can get more brand deals,' Debbie says.

'Right.' Gillian laughs.

A beat of silence.

'Well, thanks for looking after Angel. Her stuff's in the bag.' Debbie gestures towards the bag by the carrier.

'Okay,' Gillian replies.

'Well, I'll go then,' Debbie says.

'Okay,' Gillian repeats.

Debbie feels hollow. She wants her mother to want her to have a fun trip. To be excited for her. She wants to be invited to stay for a bit. To sit on the sofa. Have a cup of tea. Watch Strictly. She wants a mother who loves her, enjoys her company, and cares.

'See you later,' Debbie says as she leaves.

'See you,' Gillian replies.

Debbie closes the front door behind her and walks in a strange daze to her car.

Have a good trip, stay safe, text me when you get there. All the things normal parents might say go through her head, unspoken.

As Debbie drives home, she tries not to get too down, not to let her mother upset her. But the truth is that her mother's hit a nerve this time. Debbie *is* broke. She is in debt. And this whole influencer thing has been making less and less sense.

The money she gets from brands keeps her going, just about, but it's not enough. She needs to be doing better, making more. She hopes this holiday might help. That she might get exposure, gain more followers, and attract some higher-paying brand deals, but you never know with social media. It's all so random. So up in the air.

Debbie wonders if she should have been like Lauren. Done a law course. Got a steady office job.

Settled down in suburbia with a nice man. What's so bad about that? Why didn't she do that?

Lauren's settled. Lauren's steady. But Debbie has nothing. No home. No chance of getting one at this rate. No tangible prospects. No boyfriend. Maybe her mum's right this time. Maybe she is failing.

Maybe she should pack it all in, admit defeat. Become an accountant or something.

And yet she knows she won't. She's too addicted. She's addicted to being online. The likes. The comments. The freebies. The lottery-like rush of scoring a good brand deal. Or an all expenses paid trip. She couldn't be like Lauren even if she tried. Debbie takes a deep breath. Fuck it. Fuck her mum and fuck the misery she always seems to make her feel. She's going on this trip, and she's going to have a good time.

CHAPTER NINE

Debbie manages to get a good night's sleep, surprising herself, and she buzzes with nervous excitement as she drives through the dark streets of Brentwood at 4am to pick up Amelia.

She puts her mother out of her mind; after all, it's not like her behaviour is anything new. And she doesn't want to be negative during this trip.

Amelia is waiting outside her building with three suitcases, wearing sunglasses even though it's still dark. She looks up from her phone and waves as Debbie approaches.

The boot is already full of Debbie's luggage, so Amelia loads her cases onto the backseat.

'What's that smell?' Debbie asks as Amelia gets into the car.

Amelia smells of lavender, a bit like potpourri, and Debbie wrinkles her nose as they set off.

'Oh!' Amelia laughs awkwardly. 'It's a, erm, calming roller.'

'A what?'

Amelia retrieves the roller from her bag.

'It's a roll-ball thing; you put it on your wrists. It's essential oils, like lavender, frankincense, ylang-ylang, or something; I don't know.'

'Okay, is that, like, your new perfume?' Debbie asks, perplexed. Amelia has always been a Dior J'adore kind of girl.

'No, it's for…' Amelia trails off.

Debbie glances over at her.

'Nerves. Travel anxiety.'

'Oh.'

'I just don't love flying, that's all. Just thought I'd whack some on!' Amelia insists, with a laugh.

'Okay,' Debbie replies, winding down the window. 'Sorry hon, it smells like a bouquet in a fucking Catholic church in here.'

They join the motorway, a cool breeze blowing through the window.

Amelia flicks through the radio stations until she lands on one playing eighties classics.

'How cool would it be if they played Holiday by Madonna?' she jokes.

The radio station plays Blondie instead, and Debbie and Amelia sing along to *Atomic*, belting at the top of their lungs, their nerves giving way to excitement for their trip.

'Your hair is beautiful!' They sing, pointing at each other, laughing.

So we are proper friends, Debbie thinks as they laugh and belt along, Amelia finally out of business mode.

They stay that way—excited, giddy—as they arrive at Heathrow and make their way through airport security and Duty Free, inspecting discounts on Chanel lipsticks and top skincare.

Getting onto the plane, they both try to play it cool as they turn left to first class, a novelty for them both, despite Amelia's father's wealth.

Sky-high, they order champagne and take pictures, posing in their roomy first-class seats, and for once, their smiles are genuine. This is so much better than Luxe Americana.

They eat and watch films and gossip, and then a man sitting nearby starts snoring and muttering in his sleep. They watch him, wide-eyed. And then his hand moves down to his crotch, and he starts scratching his balls as he dreams.

At first, the girls try not to laugh, but in the end they find it so hysterical that they're crying. Maybe it's the champagne or the altitude, but they can't stop laughing. They clamp their hands over their mouths and wipe tears from their eyes. Even the air hostesses notice and giggle along too, in spite of themselves.

It occurs to Debbie that she hasn't laughed so much in ages. She's red-faced with it. Exhausted from it.

Eventually, she and Amelia also fall asleep, and by the time they wake up, the plane has landed.

CHAPTER TEN

The next few days are packed.

Debbie and Amelia start by exploring the hotel, taking pictures in its luxury spa, its mall, and its Michelin restaurants, as well as taking dozens of shots by the rooftop pool.

They tick off their contractual obligations to the hotel, getting all the pictures done, while taking hundreds more. They're like kids in a candy shop, unable to believe they're in such a lavish and luxurious place. It's every bit as good as it looked on Instagram, and their posts are getting thousands and thousands of likes.

Venturing beyond the hotel, they visit the most popular tourist attractions—the highest rated on TripAdvisor and the ones most likely to boost engagement. They pose until they get perfect shots. They dine in some of the most upscale restaurants, visit the souks, and shop at the highest-end luxury malls. Or at least they pretend to shop. They take hundreds of photos outside designer boutiques, posing, nailing the right look for Instagram.

In just two days, Debbie's follower count jumps by 16,000. Amelia's is up by 24,000. Both girls are high on dopamine, as well as the thrill of being in such a glamorous, exciting place.

They return to their hotel in the evening and lounge by the pool, wearing their best bikinis, posing with cocktails, and taking even more pictures.

As the sun goes down, they go back to their room.

Debbie orders fries from room service, while Amelia tweaks a picture on Photoshop.

There's a knock on the door.

Debbie gets up and answers. A hotel concierge stands before her. He doesn't have her fries. He's dressed immaculately with gelled, slicked back hair. There's so much gel in his hair that it looks mirror-like. Yet he's courtly and polished, like something from another century. He looks around thirty, and yet there's something about his manner that feels older to Debbie.

'Hello. I am very sorry for the interruption. I have a message from Yusef. He would like to invite you and Amelia for a getaway at an exclusive resort owned by Mirage Royale in the desert. All-expenses-paid. Several other influencers from the hotel will also be there. Here are the details.'

The concierge hands Debbie a golden envelope. It's shiny, like something from the Willy Wonka Chocolate Factory.

'Okay…'

'Please let us know by this evening if you wish to attend. The hotel will arrange the transportation.'

'Okay, will do. Thanks!'

'You're welcome. Have a wonderful evening.'

The concierge bows in a way that makes Debbie cringe. Did he learn that at some kind of hotelier training school?

Debbie smiles awkwardly and closes the door.

She turns to Amelia.

'We've been invited to the desert.'

'Yeah, I heard. Let's see.'

Debbie sits on her bed and tears open the envelope. It contains a brochure, and she flicks through it, as Amelia sits down next to her. It features glossy shots of an incredible-looking hotel, even grander and more ostentatious than Mirage Royale. A staggeringly classy mansion as opposed to a state-of-the-art skyscraper. The brochure features shots of desert safaris, too, with striking images of desert dunes, cacti, and wildlife—jackals, sand cats, antelope, and falcons. There are pictures of beaming, glamorous girls quad biking and smiling on camel rides. As well as images of an otherworldly-looking spa and exotic, ostentatious banquets laid out under the stars.

'Wow,' Amelia remarks. 'But what about our plans? The itinerary.'

'We can do half that stuff here by the looks of it. And it's all-expenses-paid, didn't you hear?'

'I guess… I just… We had a plan.'

'I know, but *look* at this place.'

'It does look nice.'

'We could get some great pics.'

Debbie can already envisage the pictures in her mind. How jaw-dropping they'd look on Instagram. A red silk gown she packed, just in case, which is vintage from eBay but looks like Valentino, would look great in the mansion's grand lobby, with her gold Massimo Dutti dupe sandals.

'Yeah, I guess,' Amelia relents.

An invite is enclosed in the brochure and in handwritten gold lettering reads, 'You are invited for an unforgettable desert experience. Leaving at 11am, Friday, from the Mirage Royale lobby.'

It's signed by Yusef.

I would love to see you there!

YF

'It's just one night. Come on, we may as well.'

'Alright then.' Amelia shrugs, giving in.

CHAPTER ELEVEN

The following day, Debbie and Amelia wheel their suitcases through reception, putting on their designer sunglasses as they step out into the luminous light.

Their car is already waiting, and they are ushered towards it by the same concierge who delivered the gold envelope. He smiles obsequiously in that over-enthusiastic way that still sets Debbie on edge. They're just girls trying to enjoy a holiday, and yet he bows whenever he sees them as though they're royalty. It makes Debbie feel weirdly self-conscious. Amelia doesn't seem to mind as much.

In fact, she hands him her phone to get a snap of her and Debbie before they set off.

'Could you take, like, ten? Maybe twenty?' She asks, laughing, trying to seem casual.

The concierge isn't at all fazed. He's used to doubling up as a photographer for influencers.

Beads of sweat crawl down Debbie's back as they pose in the sun, smiling, chests out, chins forward, trying to look as elongated and sexy and attractive as possible.

Eventually, the concierge hands Amelia her phone.

The girls inspect the pictures as their driver takes their bags, loading them into the boot of the car.

'Have a wonderful trip,' the concierge says, still smiling his full beam smile, holding the car doors open for the girls.

Debbie and Amelia thank him, and he bows once more. Debbie tries not to roll her eyes. She's itching to get away, and she's glad when he finally closes the doors. He exchanges a look with the driver and heads back into the hotel, and Debbie lets out a sigh of relief.

The car is air-conditioned and cool. It's spotlessly clean. The driver pulls away from the hotel, joining the busy traffic.

Debbie smiles at Amelia, excited, and Amelia smiles back before returning her attention to her phone.

'Send me one of those pics?' Debbie asks. 'I want to add it to Insta.'

'Sure. I'll send you the best one. I was just going to put it on stories.'

The sky is blisteringly blue above the skyscrapers as they pull away from the hotel, and everything gleams. The buildings are so tall, piercing the sky like needles, architectural marvels, not exactly beautiful, but undoubtedly impressive. Passing underneath them gives Debbie a feeling almost like vertigo, in reverse. As though the buildings could crumble at any moment, toppling like the Tower of Babel. There's something unnatural about them, and she's glad when they get further out of the city, away from the sparkling silver density, towards the suburbs, where the factories, apartment blocks, and less ostentatious shopping centres feel almost like the ones back home.

Debbie looks through the pictures Amelia has sent. They're nice. They really do look like they're having a great time. The pictures don't capture the smell of that anti-anxiety roll-on blend that Amelia is still wearing. Debbie thought it was just for travel, but Amelia has been reeking of lavender ever since they got here.

Debbie posts the best shot to her page with a caption: *Off on a desert adventure! Can't wait! #explorer #travelling #blessed.*

She looks out of the window. Huge billboards line the highway for shaving creams, perfumes, and holiday packages. The models smile in a cheesy way, and the adverts feel oddly retro, like something from the 1950s.

As they drive further and further from the city, the billboards peter out, and the factories dwindle to nothing. There are no warehouses. No blocks of flats. Nothing but a wide, empty expanse.

Messages pour in from Debbie's followers in response to her picture.

'Living the dream! Have the best time!'

'Take me with you! 😃 *'*

'Such babes! Wow!'

'Obsessed!'

There are more comments, but they won't load. Debbie looks out the window. The landscape is barren now. It's just rocky expanses and desert plains, rugged, and dry. Unbroken by buildings or human habitation.

'I'm not sure about this.' Amelia says as the road cuts through rocky plateaus and sand and cacti, and more rocks and sand and cacti, getting deeper and deeper into the wilderness.

'What do you mean?' Debbie asks casually, even though she feels a twinge of something too.

'It feels like we're getting very far from civilisation.' Whispering, Amelia adds, 'It's just you, me, and this random man.'

She flicks her eyes towards the driver.

'Well yeah, we're going to the desert! We do have to, like, go to the desert...!'

Debbie glances at the driver, his close-cropped hair, leathery face, and dark, focused eyes. A dice dangles from his rearview mirror.

'It's fine,' she adds. 'He works for the hotel.'

Amelia laughs weakly. 'I guess.'

Debbie reaches over and pats Amelia's leg.

'Just relax, babe.'

'Okay.'

Amelia turns and looks out of the window. And Debbie can tell she's really not okay.

CHAPTER TWELVE

Debbie and Amelia sink into silence as they get deeper into the desert.

The desert roads are lined on either side by dry, barren wilderness.

The colour palette of the landscape is both captivating and alien to Debbie. The rocky expanse features ripples of red, pink, orange, and yellow, beautiful, striking marbling shades, with the occasional cactus adding a pop of green. The blue sky shimmers in the background. On one level, Debbie is enchanted by the sumptuous, otherworldly shades and the unfolding, endless expanse, like nothing she's ever seen before and so different compared to England's countryside—a palette of greens that seems quaint and humdrum in comparison, and yet her appreciation of the landscape is tempered by a feeling of unease. A feeling of losing control.

Amelia looks blankly out of the window, silent. And Debbie can feel the tension radiating off her. It's in her tight posture, her detached expression.

Debbie checks her phone. Still no reception. It died a while ago. Not one bar.

She stabs at her screen, trying to refresh Instagram for the seventh or eighth time, to no avail.

The hotel will have WiFi. It's not a big deal. Surely, she can go without the internet for one car ride? They are in the desert after all.

And yet, the lack of connectivity and the mounting sense of desolation is rattling her. She finds herself looking at her mum's WhatsApp account, clicking onto her profile picture. It's wholesome. A robin she photographed in the garden. Debbie feels a pang of emotion. Somewhere between sadness and love.

She and her mum have issues, but one thing Debbie does like about her mother is her appreciation of nature.

Gillian notices things that pass Debbie by. Skylarks in spring, bluebells. She goes for long walks in the local nature reserve with her digital SLR. She reads books on photography and takes pictures of birds and flowers, uploading them to Facebook. Her pictures aren't amazing, but it's sweet.

Debbie has a strong and sudden urge to speak to her mum. To find out what she's doing. To find out how Angel is. She feels an intense longing to be home. Back in Brentwood. To be on familiar streets. The M25. With its solidity and service stations and signs that make sense.

Feeling watched, Debbie glances up to see the driver looking at her with a beady, piercing gaze. He quickly looks away, but not so quickly that Debbie fails to notice the way he's been taking her in.

Did he see the worry and anxiety wrought on her features?

Debbie edges closer to the window, out of his eyeline.

She's uneasy.

Deep down, in the pit of her stomach, she has a feeling, a horrible feeling. A feeling of dread. A question is presenting itself: what have you done?

CHAPTER THIRTEEN

The unbroken, barren desert expanse gives way to a small village: a spattering of small earthen homes with sand-coloured walls that practically blend into the desert dunes.

The driver slows. By the side of the road, a few women, with deeply wrinkled faces, cloaked in headscarves and shawls, are selling wares laid out on blankets before them. One sells wicker baskets, the other brightly coloured necklaces, bohemian wooden bead pieces that Debbie imagines would do well at a London market.

The driver stops at a drinks hut. A small shack with a rusted Coca-Cola sign and a corrugated iron roof. Debbie doubts the drinks are particularly refrigerated.

She sighs and checks her phone. Still nothing.

She looks over at Amelia, who's also jabbing at her screen.

'What are we going to do if we don't have any reception? How are we going to make any content?' Amelia says loudly.

Debbie notes that Amelia clearly wants the driver to hear and register her dissatisfaction.

'There must be some out here,' Debbie comments. 'I mean, how do people communicate?!'

She leans forward.

'Hey? Is there reception here?' She asks the driver.

His eyes swivel up, meeting hers in the rearview mirror once more. There's something in his gaze. An intensity, a watchfulness, that sets Debbie on edge.

Is he into her? What's his deal?

The last thing she needs right now in the middle of the desert is a driver who's a creep.

It's not like she's dressed immodestly. She's wearing jeans, a loose-fitting long-sleeved blouse, and her hair is tied up in a demure bun. She's not even wearing false lashes or lipstick.

And yet, Debbie isn't really sure the driver's gaze is lascivious. It's intense, as though he knows something she doesn't. His eyes linger on her for a second before he answers.

'No reception,' he says.

'There's no reception here? At all?' Amelia presses, horrified.

'No reception.'

'What the actual fuck?' Amelia spits. 'We're content creators. We produce content on our phones.' Amelia jabs at her phone. 'That's why we're here! That's the *whole point* of us being here.'

The driver doesn't respond.

'This is ridiculous. This is fucking ridiculous.'

Amelia springs out of the car, marching out, waving her phone around, trying to get a bar of reception. A few village girls run up to her and stare, as though encountering a glamorous princess, an exotic creature. Amelia tries to smile for them, but her expression is twisted and strained, and Debbie can tell she's on the verge of crying.

'We really do need our phones,' Debbie points out, keeping her voice soft and calm, taking a different approach. 'We're here for work. We were invited by Yusef. He wanted us to come so we could create content about the hotel and this amazing part of the world to help promote it. But if there's no reception here, that's going to make things difficult. Are you sure?'

'Yes, I am sure. There's no reception here,' the driver says again. He holds his own phone up, waving it as though to illustrate his point.

Except, as he places it back down, Debbie notices the screen flash. A message.

'You just got a message,' Debbie remarks, pointing at his screen.

The driver looks at his phone.

'Text message.'

'You have reception!'

'No internet. Phone reception.'

'But we have nothing!'

'I am on local network,' the man says.

'We are too. Our providers set it up.'

The driver shrugs, his face a picture of cluelessness.

'I don't know.'

Debbie jabs at her phone again and groans. She looks to Amelia, who is holding hers up to the sky while the village girls tug at the hem of her skirt, pawing at her handbag.

Amelia turns around, clearly irritated, and comes back to the car.

'Nothing. Not one bar. We can't be here if we have no internet.'

The driver doesn't respond. He gets out of the car and heads to the drinks hut.

'What the fuck?' Amelia groans.

Debbie smiles awkwardly. She can't help noticing how quickly their mask of civility falls away the moment their internet connection drops. They're both addicts. Plugged into the net like junkies to smack.

Debbie wonders what it would be like if the internet just stopped. Stopped completely, and the analogue age returned. No social media. No messaging. No apps. Just people, existing, inhabiting their communities, meeting each other without being able to scan profiles, without being able to follow. It seems so strange to think it was just one generation before her. It feels like a whole other world.

And yet it's one Debbie's wondered about. Social media is her job; it's given her everything she has, and yet she sometimes suspects it's done the world more harm than good. Perhaps those men in her 'Fucking Assholes' folder, for example, might not be so bad if they didn't have the internet at their fingertips: limitless opportunities for temptation and transgression. Perhaps without the net, they might spend more time with their partners and value what they have.

Debbie thinks about all the friends she has online. The likes that pour in daily. All the social media girls who call her 'babe' and 'hon' and message her like they care, who she's never even met. Will likely never meet.

Without social media, maybe she'd feel less lonely for once.

'Let's just go back,' Amelia says. 'We can't be here without the internet. We can't do our work. This isn't what we agreed to. If I'd known there was no reception out here, I wouldn't have come.'

Debbie knows Amelia is right. Not having reception is going to make things difficult, but the mansion will surely have WiFi. They can still take pictures, do activities, snap everything, and upload shots in the evenings. And even if the internet is patchy while they're out here, a two-day digital detox might be nice. In theory, at least. The driver with his weird looks and the feeling Debbie has of losing her bearings isn't making the prospect particularly appealing.

She can't even message her mum to let her know where she is. Not that her mum really demands updates.

The driver gets back in the car, his forehead beading with sweat. He cracks open a bottle of Sprite.

'Can we go back, please?' Amelia asks him. 'We want to go back to the city. No more desert. We want to go home.'

'No! No going back. I take you to the mansion.' The driver takes a swig of his Sprite.

'No! We don't want to go to the mansion,' Amelia enunciates pointedly, irritably. 'Take us back to the city.'

'No. Mansion. Desert.'

'What the fuck?' Amelia turns to Debbie, a horrified expression on her face. 'He's forcing us to go to this fucking place!'

'Maybe he doesn't understand,' Debbie reasons.

'It's not that complicated!' Amelia protests.

The driver starts the engine, pulling away from the hut. He drives further along the desert road.

'Oh my God,' Amelia gasps. 'We're being kidnapped.'

Amelia rattles the door handle, only to find it's locked.

'We've been locked in. We've been fucking locked in.'

Amelia's face flushes, her eyes are wide, pupils like black moons, glossy. Debbie can tell she's about to cry.

Debbie can't quite figure out if Amelia is overreacting, not being much of a traveller, or if this could indeed be the start of something more troubling. The driver doesn't seem to be listening to them, that's for sure. They're cruising through vast, unfamiliar terrain, and they have no way of letting anyone know where they are. Absolutely no way.

Debbie checks her door handle too. The doors of the car have definitely been locked.

Debbie leans forward.

The driver swigs at his Sprite, sunlight falling on his face, as though he doesn't have a care in the world.

'Look, take us back to the hotel. We'll pay you,' Debbie suggests.

'No. Yusef paid me to take you to the mansion,' the driver insists.

'We'll pay you more to take us back,' Amelia counters. 'We'll pay whatever you want.'

'No,' the driver says, looking ahead.

Amelia starts to cry and whimper.

'Take us back,' she begs. 'Please just take us back.'

The driver doesn't respond.

Debbie reaches over and squeezes Amelia's hand. Her palm is sweaty.

'It'll be okay,' Debbie says, not sure she believes it.

CHAPTER FOURTEEN

'Take us back. Take us back. I'm going to complain to the hotel. I'm going to fucking sue. You have no right. This is imprisonment. This is illegal!' Amelia insists, over and over.

She's been complaining at the driver for at least ten minutes now, but he doesn't care. He doesn't even react. He just glides along the desert road, unphased. A little bored even.

Amelia stabs at her phone as he follows the road up a rocky incline.

Debbie looks out of the car window, taking in the desert expanse from a higher vantage point, craggy Jurassic-like plateaus, an endless horizon of sandy dunes.

Debbie is somewhere between denial and panic.

She keeps telling herself this is fine, that Amelia is overreacting. The driver isn't communicating with them because he doesn't have good English, surely. She keeps thinking about the brochure with its dazzling pictures, and all the girls on Instagram who rave about their trips to Yusef's hotel. Yes, this is a bit unnerving. Yes, it feels weird to be somewhere so remote, in a locked car, with a strange man, but life isn't a horror film. This isn't Hollywood. Most people aren't unhinged psychopaths. It will all be fine.

The sun glitters in the sky and as they reach the top of the rocky hill, the village shops and children are dots.

The driver flicks his indicator, its ticking noise the only sound he's emitted for a while.

He pulls off down a side road. Debbie spots the mansion from the brochure in the distance, higher up the hill. It looks just as fairytale-like in reality as it appeared in the brochure. An opulent castle-like place with a domed roof, its beauty made even more exaggerated by its incongruity with this dry, arid place. And yet despite its charm, it makes Debbie's stomach squirm.

'We're here now. There must be WiFi inside,' Debbie tells Amelia.

Amelia doesn't respond.

The driver draws to a halt outside the mansion's gates. They're large, heavy and imposing.

He presses a buzzer, and after a moment, the gates open.

Debbie notes the mansion's gates are the sort that would be impossible to climb over. A spiked edge runs across the top of them, subtle, only noticeable if you were looking.

On the other side of the gate is another winding path, leading to the house.

'I want to go home,' Amelia says, softly, to herself.

The path is lined with palm trees.

As they get closer, Debbie takes in the mansion's tall marble pillars, gold latticed windows and domed roof like the Taj Mahal.

Around twenty cars are parked in its car park. Debbie notices the Lamborghinis, Ferraris, Maseratis.

The entrance is flanked by two guards, each with guns at their side.

'What the fuck?'

'They had guns at our other hotel too,' Debbie reasons, even though the security guards with guns in the city somehow felt far less intimating there than they do here.

'I don't know why you're so relaxed about this Debbie. It's almost like you want to get raped and murdered in the middle of nowhere.'

Debbie rolls her eyes.

Yusef emerges from the mansion, wearing a huge, welcoming smile, just like the one in his picture on the hotel's Instagram page.

Amelia's eyes are watery, her cheeks blotchy, her makeup tear-streaked. Debbie tries to settle the tension on her own face, painting on a smile. Yusef looks happy, normal. Maybe this whole thing could be okay after all.

The driver releases the central locking. Amelia immediately reaches for the door handle and rushes out, like an animal fleeing captivity.

Debbie follows, glancing at the driver, who's still eyeing her in that strange, knowing way. Debbie gets out of the car with a shudder.

'Hello ladies. It's a pleasure to meet you. How was your drive?' Yusef asks.

'Not the best! We've been locked in the car against our wishes. It's been an absolute violation of our rights. We have no reception. We can't update our families, or our followers. I want to go back, right away,' Amelia insists.

Debbie notes how anger makes Amelia so much posher. She's speaking like the Queen.

'Sorry, but I really want to go back,' Amelia adds, eyes filling with tears once more.

Yusef looks taken aback.

Debbie smiles awkwardly.

She doesn't know how to feel. The script of this day is all muddled.

'I am sorry you were not warned about the reception issues in the desert. I can see how this would have been very distressing for you. We have WiFi inside the house, would you like to connect inside?'

Amelia looks at him, both wary and hopeful.

'I need to message my mum and dad,' she says.

'Of course. Come this way. We'll get that sorted right away.'

Yusef ushers the girls towards the mansion.

It's undeniably beautiful, and they fall into an awkward silence, begrudgingly taking in the plush spectacle of this extraordinary place.

Debbie shoots Amelia a gentle, encouraging smile, but Amelia glares back.

The guards, flanked with huge guns—Debbie isn't sure what, AK47s?—eye the girls as they walk up the steps to the entrance.

Amelia walks slowly, and Debbie can sense her trepidation.

They enter an enormous lobby with a shining marble floor threaded with gold and a winding staircase. Debbie has seen pictures of the lobby in the brochure, but it's far more striking in real life, with light falling through a vast glass atrium and shimmering, diamond-like over the space. Breathing in the scent of jasmine, Debbie takes in the carved alabaster pillars framing the space, each one etched with filigree. The lobby is so different from the vast desert plains, the jagged rocky landscape outside, and the run-down village that it's almost jarring.

'Wow,' Debbie remarks, before she even has time to think. 'This is incredible.'

Yusef smiles proudly.

'Thank you.'

Amelia stays quiet. She diverts her attention from the gleaming space and focuses on her phone.

'WiFi Royale?'

'Yes, that is correct,' Yusef confirms.

'And the password?'

'Marana.'

'Marana,' Amelia echoes. 'Whatever that means.'

She types in the password and sighs with relief in a way that indicates to Debbie that she's definitely connected. She starts typing a message.

'Let me show you around,' Yusef says.

A few hotel concierges enter the lobby, carrying Debbie and Amelia's bags.

Yusef gestures for Debbie to follow him down a corridor.

'Are you coming?' Debbie asks Amelia, who's engrossed in her phone.

'What?'

'Yusef wants to show us around.'

'No, I'm alright.'

'Okay.'

Debbie gives Yusef an apologetic look, ashamed at how ungrateful Amelia is being.

Yusef appears unruffled and smiles warmly.

'This is such a beautiful place,' Debbie says, partly to be nice and partly because it's true. 'I've never seen anything like it in my life.'

'Thank you. It's a labour of love. I opened this place at the same time as the hotel, but it's more off the beaten track. I don't publicise it as much, but I put just as much care and attention into it, if not more.'

'I can tell. Both are beautiful, but this is otherworldly.'

Yusef smiles, a genuine smile that reaches his eyes, and Debbie can tell he's pleased.

She glances over her shoulder at Amelia in the distance, typing on her phone.

'Sorry about Amelia. She's not used to being away from home. I think this is all a bit much for her.'

'It's not a problem. I'm used to nervous travellers.'

Debbie smiles. Normality is returning. Everything is starting to feel okay again.

Yusef shows her the palatial dining room, the gorgeous spa, the enormous pool, the vast library, and the lounge, where he invites her to take a seat and enjoy some fresh mint tea and baklava.

'Please, be my guest,' he says, gesturing towards the table.

Debbie sits down, grateful, bashful. Yusef reminds her a bit of the concierge back at Mirage Royale. He has that same obsequious, eager-to-please manner.

'I'll see if Amelia would like to join you,' Yusef suggests.

'Okay,' Debbie replies. 'Shall I come?'

'No, don't worry. Tuck in, as they say in England.'

Debbie laughs and reaches for a sandwich as Yusef heads back to the lobby. She lets out a breath she hadn't realised she was holding and reaches for a perfect cheese and cucumber sandwich with crisp, sharp edges.

She contemplates waiting for Amelia, but her stomach rumbles, and she takes a bite.

The sandwich is delicious. The best, most perfect cheese and cucumber sandwich she's ever had, the quintessential English classic, all the way out here, so far, far away.

It occurs to her that she hasn't taken a picture. For the first time in months, she forgot about social media. She starts snapping the spread. She posts a story on Instagram of the elegant lounge, her hand picking up a gold teapot, pouring a cup of mint tea.

She flicks her camera into selfie mode, but her face is shiny, her makeup smudged, and imperfect.

She takes her face powder from her bag and touches up her makeup, adding a slick of lip gloss, which she slides back into her bag as Yusef returns, with Amelia walking a few paces behind him, head bowed, like a naughty child.

Amelia clocks the spread. Debbie smiles.

Amelia looks a little sheepish.

'Thanks,' she says, awkwardly, as Yusef gestures for her to take a seat.

'Make yourself at home. When you have eaten, we will show you to your room. I'll be next door, enjoy.'

'Thank you,' Amelia repeats.

Amelia watches Yusef walk away.

'You okay?' Debbie asks.

Amelia shrugs.

'Not really. I'm going back tomorrow, I don't care. I asked Yusef, and he said it was fine. I feel too far away, it's freaking me out. I still don't know quite where we are. No one will fucking tell me. It's just "the desert", as if that means anything.'

'I think it's fine. I mean, this place is incredible. And look at this…' Debbie gestures at the spread. 'I think our driver was just weird, but it'll be cool. We'll meet the other girls at dinner. We're going to have fun here. We just need to relax.'

'Yeah, that would be easier to do if I could tell my parents where the hell I am,' Amelia comments.

Debbie looks at her phone: 38 notifications. People are liking her story.

She realises one is about a picture Amelia has posted. Debbie clicks on it. It's a selfie taken in the lobby. Amelia looks pretty, head tilted, eyes sparkling. She's refreshed her makeup, and she looks like she's having the time of her life despite everything.

'Wow.' Debbie flicks her phone round to Amelia. 'You really know how to turn it on, don't you?'

Amelia shrugs. 'Wasn't going to miss that backdrop.'

Debbie laughs. 'Fair enough.'

Debbie puts her own camera in selfie mode and starts recording.

'Hey guys! We've just arrived for our desert getaway. Check out the beautiful place we're staying at. It's absolutely *stunning*.'

Debbie pans around the room.

'Still with the gorgeous Amelia, and we're about to tuck into an incredible cream tea.'

Amelia gives a wave, automatically turning on the Insta-charm.

'Probably the best I've ever seen, halfway around the world! Ironic, huh? Anyway, which cake do you think I should start with? They all look *so* delicious!'

Debbie pans across the cake selection.

'I think I might go for a Victoria sponge, a classic!'

Debbie picks up a perfectly dusted finger of sponge and takes a bite, eating as tenderly and as prettily as she can.

'Oh wow, that was good! So good. Be right back; just got to have a few more!'

She clicks off.

'Wow, that really was good,' Debbie remarks, looking down at the sponge. 'Are you going to have some?'

'I guess,' Amelia replies.

She plucks a few cakes from the display and places them on her plate, along with a few sandwiches.

'They do look nice,' she admits, although her tone is glum.

'What's up?'

'I just didn't think it would be like this. I expected somewhere a bit more central. Part of a touristy area, you know? I'm just creeped out.'

'This is just travel, Amelia. It's unnerving. You've got to relax, roll with it.'

'Debbie, you went to Thailand for like a month in your gap year, you're hardly Bear Grylls,' Amelia points out, smirking.

'Hey, I went to other places too, like Portugal and, um, Cyprus.'

'Doesn't really count. Can you take a picture of me?'

Amelia hands Debbie her phone, and she poses with a cup of mint tea as though she's not desperate to be anywhere other than here.

CHAPTER FIFTEEN

After tea, a concierge shows Debbie and Amelia to their room.

The winding staircase in the lobby leads to a long corridor flanked by suites.

The décor of the rooms isn't dissimilar to Mirage Royale. The plush, ostentatious feel of the first floor of the mansion is replaced with a more simplified, modern look. Like their room in the city, the room the girls are staying in features twin beds, a big TV, an ensuite, and a massive plate glass window. Yet unlike their room at Mirage Royale, the view beyond the window is of a rocky horizon and dusty dunes.

The concierge places the girls' bags down, leaving them to 'settle in.'.

Debbie glances at Amelia, who still looks uneasy, despite having calmed down somewhat over tea.

Debbie runs her fingertips over the marble dressing table, which is shiny and spotless, just like the one at Mirage Royale.

The sound of the concierge's footsteps fades as he retreats down the hall.

'So, are you okay now? It's not that bad, right?' Debbie asks.

Amelia looks out over the desert.

In the distance, desert winds whip rivulets of sand up into the air, like miniature tornadoes.

Amelia doesn't know what to say.

The truth is, Amelia wants to go home. There's a strange feeling in her stomach, a sense of alarm deep within, a fear bubbling away, telling her to leave, to get away from this place. But she knows she can't.

The driver won't drive her back, that much is clear. She's not going to be able to leave until tomorrow, it seems. Even if she tried to leave of her own accord, the security guards with their guns might not let her walk freely. And even if she did manage to get out of here, she'd be stranded. She doesn't have reception to call for a taxi, and with the language barrier, she couldn't ask any of the locals for help. She'd be lost in the desert, facing a different kind of danger.

The unease is real, palpable, but Amelia has decided to shut herself off to it for now. Take pictures, pretend. An extreme version of what she always does.

Another Lamborghini arrives in the car park.

'Who do you think those cars belong to?' Amelia asks, turning to look at Debbie, who's admiring her reflection in the mirror.

Debbie comes over and looks out of the window, taking in the extraordinarily expensive cars parked outside the mansion. Debbie's pretty sure there are more now than when they first arrived.

'The other girls' maybe? Yusef's collection?'

'Hmm...'

Debbie turns away from the window and heaves her suitcase onto the bed. She unzips it and starts unpacking her things.

Amelia slumps on the bed. She has no intention of unpacking and scrolls on her phone instead.

The room phone rings.

'Yusef wants a chit chat.' Amelia rolls her eyes.

Debbie takes it.

'We're organising a quad biking trip to the desert before it gets dark,' Yusef says. 'Some of the other guests, also influencers, are already there. A few are heading out now. Would you and Amelia care to join?'

'Sounds great. One second.'

Debbie cups her hand over the receiver as she asks Amelia.

'We only just got here,' Amelia protests.

'It would be good for pictures.'

Amelia sighs. 'Okay, fine.'

'Sure, we'll come.'

'Great. It's in half an hour. Just make your way to reception.'

Debbie thanks Yusef and ends the call.

'We're not going to have reception out there, are we?' Amelia grumbles.

'Probably not,' Debbie admits. 'We don't have to be connected *all* the time.'

'I know,' Amelia sighs.

'You're addicted.'

'I'm not, I just…'

'You're out of your comfort zone.'

'I suppose so. Yeah, you could call it that.'

'Come on, let's just try to have fun. Next week we're going to be back in boring Brentwood. If we don't make the most of this now, we'll be kicking ourselves.'

'Okay.'

So the girls get ready. Debbie finds a zip bag containing her quad biking outfit: black leggings, a matching long-sleeved top, a bandana, Ray-Ban aviators. She even has a scrunchie that goes with her bandana.

Amelia gets ready too, but her outfit is a little less thought out. Just leggings and a t-shirt. Debbie's surprised. Amelia normally always makes an effort.

'Aren't you dressing up?' Debbie asks, confused.

'I am,' Amelia replies, with a secretive glint in her eye.

Debbie doesn't get a chance to find out what Amelia means before they head down to reception.

CHAPTER SIXTEEN

As the girls get into the car once more, three more vehicles arrive. A Porsche and two more Ferraris.

A few men get out, dressed in suits, their drivers retrieving their bags from the back.

They're in their fifties, sixties perhaps. Unremarkable-looking bar the wealth demonstrated through their impeccable clothing, designer sunglasses, and expensive luggage.

Debbie watches as Yusef emerges from the hotel to greet them with that warm, welcoming smile and his trademark expansive pose.

So these men are staying at the mansion too. Are they on holiday? Debbie wonders. She thought this place was exclusive, invite-only, a private resort owned by Yusef, not a hotel for the general public.

Why would men like this, businessmen by the looks of it, want to visit the desert anyway? What's here for them? The mansion is far away from any business districts. And Debbie can hardly imagine these men have come all this way to go quad biking or embark on a desert safari.

It seems a little odd, but Debbie decides not to overthink it. Their lives have nothing to do with her. And perhaps they know Yusef; perhaps they're associates of his. It's really none of her business.

Debbie averts her gaze and spots a lizard lounging by a tree, looking like a miniature crocodile, scaly and khaki-coloured. Its eyes meet Debbie's. She feels a sense of childlike wonder as she holds eye contact with this strange reptilian creature.

'Look!' She reaches to Amelia, taps her arm and points, but by the time Amelia looks over, the lizard has shrunk out of sight, slipping into the shadows under the ferns, and the car pulls away.

It doesn't take long to get lost once more in the desert. Endless sandy plains stretch far and wide. Now that the panic has faded, Debbie contemplates the landscape. The sandy dunes, sculpted by the wind, are a changing landscape like nothing she's ever witnessed before. So different from Brentwood with its little tarmacked roads and shops and suburbia. The contours of this place can change daily. Fierce winds can remodel it. There's something beguiling about that elasticity, something elemental. Debbie notices that some of the dunes have ripples in them from the winds, like waves frozen in time.

After a ten-minute drive, they arrive at a quad biking centre.

Debbie and Amelia get out of the car and are greeted by a smiling man who introduces himself as Ahmed, the owner. He hands them helmets and asks if they've ever ridden a quad bike before. Neither have. He shows them to some bikes and explains how to ride them.

They have a few test runs, and then once Ahmed's confident the girls can ride safely, they set off on their own, cruising over the desert dunes, under the blistering, shimmering sky.

There's something undeniably exciting and freeing about cruising across the desert, and despite the stress of the trip, the girls find themselves smiling, laughing, and letting go. They pass some other girls around their age, who must also be guests of Yusef, and they wave, grinning, relieved to see women like them in this remote place.

'Let's stop over here,' Amelia suggests, looking over her shoulder, making sure she's out of sight from the quad biking centre.

'Okay,' Debbie replies, assuming they're going to take pictures.

But then Amelia pulls off her top, revealing a gold Dolce & Gabbana bikini top.

'Take my picture,' she says, urgency in her voice, knowing she shouldn't be revealing so much skin in public over here.

Now Debbie understands why she didn't dress up.

Debbie eyes her a little jealously. She looks incredible, her long dark hair billowing on the desert breeze.

Amelia poses, catching the light, and Debbie snaps shot after shot of Amelia looking sexy and standout in this arid, exotic place.

A quad bike approaches.

'Shit.' Amelia puts her top back on.

As the bike approaches, it turns out to be another girl, around their age, who introduces herself as Svetlana. She's a model from Moscow. Taking in her high cheekbones, dazzling blue eyes, and a slender, perfect body, it's not hard for Debbie to believe.

Svetlana is textbook beautiful, like she's stepped off the cover of Vogue. And yet she has a striking pink streak cutting through her blonde hair and exaggeratedly fake breasts that Debbie feels detract from her beauty somewhat. Friendly and exuberant, Svetlana explains that she's staying at the mansion, too, and that she came alone.

Unlike Debbie and Amelia, she seems completely okay with being out here in the middle of nowhere, completely unbothered by the remoteness. She seems excited by the whole experience.

Debbie wonders if maybe she and Amelia have been being paranoid.

'Shall I take your picture? You two together?' Svetlana offers.

Debbie and Amelia smile and wrap their arms around each other's shoulders, while Svetlana snaps away.

And for the briefest moment, their trip feels like a normal girl's holiday, a wild, fun adventure.

In a few years' time, Debbie will delete the pictures, finding that she's unable to look at them without feeling a pang of deep pain and loss.

CHAPTER SEVENTEEN

Yusef has invited you for dinner in the main hall at 8pm.

Amelia sneers at the note.

'Can't we just order room service or something? I'm not really in the mood for dinner with Yusef.'

Debbie looks around the room for a menu, something about room service, but there's nothing.

'It's probably not actually dinner with him. He's just letting us know that dinner is at eight.'

'Maybe,' Amelia replies glumly.

Debbie can tell from the shadows under Amelia's eyes, which her Touch Eclat is struggling to conceal, that she's tired. And it's not just tiredness from the quad biking, it's exhaustion from being here. From this trip. From being so far from home.

Amelia is putting on a brave face to get content, to get the most out of this trip, but she's not really enjoying herself. She's not really relaxed.

'Let's just go. I'm hungry,' Debbie comments.

'This place is so weird. Like, quad biking was cool and everything, but I don't like this whole "do this, do that, come here" vibe. At least back in the city we had some freedom. It felt like we were actually on holiday. This is so controlled. It's like a weird, creepy school trip.'

'Yeah, I know,' Debbie admits. 'But we can leave tomorrow, can't we? It's just one more night.'

'I suppose.'

The girls take showers, washing away the sand that clings to their skin, their scalps, even the crevices of their ears.

'Shall we get dressed up?' Debbie suggests. 'It's hardly dinner at the Travel Lodge. We can get some really good shots.'

'Yeah, I guess so,' Amelia agrees.

Debbie is glad she had the forethought to pack eveningwear. She finds the zip bag containing her Valentino-like dress.

Amelia gets ready too, having also prepared. She puts on a cute Chloé dress, her usual Cartier bangles, Jimmy Choos. She applies make-up, winged eyeliner and long lashes, getting into it, steadying her nerves and anxiety with the familiar routine of make-up application. She borrows Debbie's perfume, Flower Bomb by Viktor & Rolf, and the room is heady with it.

As the girls get ready, they post selfies, acting like they're having the time of their lives.

'It's annoying that we can't get any drinks sent up here,' Amelia sighs as she taps on her phone. 'Wow, my desert shot's got 11,816 likes! That's my best for months!'

'That's awesome, babe,' Debbie replies.

She checks the picture she's posted of her quad biking, which has 3,298 likes, and she can't help feeling irritated. Amelia always trumps her, no matter how hard she tries. Why didn't she pack a bikini for the desert?

Amelia doesn't ask about Debbie's shot. Perhaps she already knows it's not performed as well and doesn't want to make her awkward. Or perhaps she hasn't checked.

'Let's just eat, take some photos, and come straight back to the room,' Amelia suggests as they make their way downstairs.

'Sounds like a plan,' Debbie says.

Debbie finds herself hoping Yusef isn't at dinner. Something about him niggles at her. He seems nice, but he's a little too nice. It's not that Debbie expects people to be genuine; nearly everyone in the Instagram and PR world is fake to some degree, but there's something about Yusef that unsettles her, and she can't quite put her finger on what it is. Debbie doesn't want to mention it to Amelia. Amelia is put out enough. And anyway, the thought makes Debbie feel ungrateful, paranoid even. Yusef has been nothing but welcoming and accommodating. He's gifted her and Amelia with an incredibly luxurious holiday, one of the most lavish she's ever experienced. She can hardly hold the fact that he seems a bit fake against him.

But when they reach the main hall, and Yusef greets them, and the room is half full of influencers like them and half full of businessmen at least twenty years older, Debbie starts to trust her instincts about Yusef after all. He's not as nice as he seems.

An enormous dining table is laid out with place settings, ensuring older businessmen flank young women.

Yusef leads Debbie and Amelia to their seats. They're seated next to each other, but on either side is an older man.

Debbie and Amelia exchange a look.

One man scrolls on his phone, not glancing up.

The other studiously tucks into a bowl of peanuts.

Neither seems particularly interested in the girls, but the situation is unnerving.

Debbie has been invited for dinners with older men more times than she can count. They slide into her DMs, compliment her, ask if she'd like to accompany them to dinner, suggesting the finest restaurants in London.

They often insist that all they want is dinner with a pretty girl, nothing else. They offer huge sums.

Often the requests seem dodgy, from anonymous-looking pages, but sometimes they come from men whose profiles look legit and whose identities check out.

They really do seem to work at the fancy banks or companies they claim to. They just have no shame when it comes to making seedy requests to women online.

A couple of times, Debbie has agreed to these dinners. Dinner and nothing else.

The last time, a year or so ago, she was taken out by a man in his sixties, who had just launched a tech start-up. He lived in Hampshire but was in London a lot. He was feeling pumped, emboldened, having left his job to pursue a new venture as an 'entrepreneur'. He wanted a beautiful girl to talk about himself to.

He seemed harmless. Sad and a bit pathetic, sure, but he didn't seem like he'd try anything on.

Debbie insisted before they met that she wasn't an escort and there would be no extras, just dinner, and he assured her that was all he wanted.

So they met at a wine bar and then went on to dinner.

Debbie may not have been a prostitute, but she felt like one. All night, she could feel people looking at them. This young girl, dressed up, with a man old enough to be her father, her grandfather even.

The man, Johnathan, didn't hit on her, just like he promised. He wasn't sleazy, but he was creepy.

He couldn't take his eyes off her. He was pasty-faced from too much time spent behind a computer, with crinkled, beady eyes. Debbie felt like she was under a microscope, like he was taking in every detail of her. Filing it away. She was Youth, Beauty and Womanhood, and he was drinking her in.

He didn't touch her, but she still felt oddly defiled.

She felt a bit sorry for him. He was clearly lonely, lost. Desperate for company.

Debbie bought a Tiffany necklace with some of the money he paid her and yet she could never bring herself to wear it. It always reminded her of that night and the sad, hopeless feeling she'd had around Johnathan. She ended up selling it on eBay.

And now here she is, being seated next to a creepy older man, who she's no doubt expected to talk to and be nice to, all for free.

Debbie rolls her eyes at Amelia. She glances around the table.

The place settings are all broken up: pretty girls, businessmen, pretty girls, businessmen, etcetera.

Debbie has been trying not to feel pissed off ever since she got to the desert. She's been trying to feel grateful, optimistic, appreciative of the opportunity, but she's irritated now, and she's clearly not alone.

Amelia leans towards her.

'What the fuck?' she hisses in her ear. 'This is some sugar daddy shit.'

'I know,' Debbie admits.

A waiter fills their glasses with champagne.

Debbie picks up her glass and takes a big sip.

Some of the girls are already entertaining the men seated next to them, laughing at their jokes, gazing at them.

Debbie is perplexed. Why are they bothering?

They don't owe these men anything. They don't owe them charm.

Some of the girls are young, young enough that being naïve would be a reasonable excuse. But others are Debbie and Amelia's age, if not older, and they too are entertaining the men seated next to them, giving them attention, listening with open, sweet expressions to whatever tedious stuff they're saying.

The waiters serve starters. Smoked salmon mousse with pretty slices of cucumber carved into flower shapes.

The food is immaculate, artful, and Debbie can't help admiring it.

She tucks in, realising all of a sudden how hungry she is.

The quad biking was surprisingly tiring, and the day has been draining in general.

She and Amelia discuss the food, avoiding the strange men beside them.

A waiter hovers nearby and tops up their champagne.

Debbie keeps drinking.

'Fabulous food, isn't it?' The man sitting next to her says.

Debbie looks at him with a sense of dread.

'Yes,' she replies blankly.

The man looks quite harmless. He's small with an unthreatening build. His face is saggy and non-descript and reminds Debbie vaguely of a worm. The expression in his eyes seems ordinary, benign. Debbie notes he's wearing a wedding ring.

'Probably the best food I've had since I got here,' he says.

'Yes, it's nice,' Debbie replies.

The man introduces himself. His name's Nigel.

Debbie gives her name with a tight smile.

Nigel asks if she's tried any of the local speciality dishes. Debbie replies, and before she knows it, she's having a conversation.

Amelia kicks her leg.

Debbie turns to her.

'Wonder what the main course is going to be!' Amelia says to her, trying to break up Debbie's chat.

'I hear it's duck,' Nigel says, butting in. 'Confit of duck, I think.'

Amelia smiles weakly.

The man seated next to her keeps looking her way, too, clearly wanting to engage, but Amelia ignores him, studiously focusing on her food. She just wants to eat and get out of here, and it's obvious for anyone to see.

Maybe it's the champagne, or maybe it's the fact that Nigel doesn't seem too bad, but strangely, Debbie finds herself loosening up.

She has an odd desire to know what Nigel's doing here. If he's working locally. What drew him to this strange mansion in the middle of nowhere.

'I'm old friends with Yusef,' Nigel explains. 'I'm here on business.'

'What do you do?'

'I work in finance.'

Debbie frowns.

'So, you're a banker…?'

'Something like that.'

'Okay…' Debbie replies, wondering why Nigel's being so vague.

'What do you do?' Nigel asks her.

'I'm an influencer,' Debbie replies, bored now.

'Well, everyone here seems to be an influencer!' Nigel laughs. 'I mean, what are your passions? Your dreams?'

Debbie shuts down, not interested.

She looks further along the table. There's a woman, around thirty perhaps, pretty in a girl-next-door way, wearing a dress Debbie has had her eye on for a while. A Prada one, orange and strapless, with jewel embellishments around the bodice. She's laughing while sipping on a glass of champagne, throwing her head back, chatting to the man next to her. She looks like she's having a really good time, which Debbie finds perplexing.

Feeling someone looking her way, Debbie looks across the table and sees a man with dark eyes staring at her, intently. He's not even bothering to be subtle. He takes a sip from his drink and just looks. Debbie smiles awkwardly but the man doesn't react. He's wearing a necklace with a big silver pendant. Debbie can't make out what the pendant is, but the necklace looks strange against his crisp white shirt. Debbie keeps expecting the man to divert his gaze, but he doesn't. He just keeps staring. Debbie rolls her eyes. *What the fuck?*

She looks away, at a blonde girl, a few seats along, barely eighteen, who's telling a man in his sixties how she wants to be a singer. Debbie cringes as the girl talks about the talent school she's attending.

Debbie notices another girl, on the other side of Nigel, talking about her modelling dreams.

What is this? It's like the men are following some kind of script, trying to get the girls to open up.

Weirdly, the men all seem to be drinking orange juice and what looks like glasses of milk. And yet the girls are on champagne. Debbie notes the men exchanging looks here and there across the table, smirking, as though they know each other. As though this is part of some joke to them.

94

Beyond the dining table, Debbie spots security guards she hadn't noticed before, standing by the doors, with guns. Security at the entrance of the place is one thing, but here, at dinner?

Fuck.

Lightheaded, Debbie gets up and excuses herself.

She makes her way to the doors, asking the guards where the ladies are, trying not to look at their guns, trying not to look scared. One of them escorts her down the hall to a bathroom and waits outside.

In a plush, pearlescent bathroom that smells like jasmine—the hotel's signature scent?— Debbie leans against the sink and tries to draw in air. Her lungs have shrunk like deflated balloons that won't inflate. They're sticky, stuck.

She hasn't had this for years: a panic attack.

They were so common during her school years that she thought they were normal. She thought maybe everyone had moments when their lungs stopped working.

It was only when she was older, and had left school, and they stopped happening quite so often that Debbie realised they weren't normal after all.

Debbie sits down on the toilet seat, head in her hands.

Breathe.

Breathe.

Just breathe.

Debbie thinks of the girls opening up about their dreams, the men drinking juice and fucking milk while the girls have champagne. She thinks about the atmosphere in the room, the conspiratorial glances between the men, the guileless women. Predators and prey. Debbie knows something bad is happening, but she's not sure exactly what.

Are these just older men wanting to be around pretty girls, or is this something darker?

Debbie tries to breathe. Her lungs squeak. She *needs* to breathe.

She thinks about Angel. Angel's soft fur. Angel's big round eyes. She thinks of going home. Her bed.

She wishes she had some Propranolol. She used to carry it around with her everywhere for moments like this, just in case. But she doesn't have any here; she hasn't needed it for years.

Gradually, she starts to breathe.

She thinks about the question Nigel asked, about her dream.

She thinks about the degree she started when she was eighteen at Edinburgh, a BSc in Psychology. Back then, she had dreams of doing a PhD, working for a university, leading a quiet, bookish, understated life. Having a little house, a nice partner.

But ironically, she stopped being bookish at university. She partied all the time. She jumped from boyfriend to boyfriend and got some modelling jobs. And after a while, she was barely going to lectures. She started her Instagram account and it was doing well. She wanted to be in London for parties and brand work, so she just left. She left university and moved back home. She thought it was a win at the time. She had a flurry of work, and then the buzz wore off, and she realised what she'd done.

She's always kicked herself for that. Late at night, she thinks about the version of herself that didn't drop out of university. A version that might still be living in Edinburgh, doing a PhD, that might have a wholesome boyfriend and a respectable life.

Debbie finds herself gasping again and shuts down her thoughts.

CHAPTER EIGHTEEN

There's a knock on the girls' door.

Debbie looks at the time on her phone: 2.04am.

She doesn't move. She got through dinner fairly monosyllabically, and she and Amelia managed to take some decent pictures in the lobby. They posted the shots to Instagram, and the likes have been pouring in. Everyone seems blown away by the opulence—this place is a far cry from Brentwood—and the enthusiastic comments have gone some way towards lifting the girls' spirits.

They went to bed, and Debbie has been trying to sleep. But deep down, she knew the night wasn't over. Even so, she still wants to deny this is happening. She still wants the script of this trip to be benign. Despite all the evidence to the contrary. Debbie hopes whoever is on the other side of the door will just go away. But she knows they won't.

A beat passes, and there's another knock. Louder this time.

'What the…' Amelia stirs.

'Leave it,' Debbie whispers. 'It's probably just some drunk creep looking for a hook-up.'

The knocking intensifies. Both girls stay quiet.

Knock. Knock. Knock.

'This is ridiculous. I'm going to tell them to piss off.' Amelia gets out of bed.

'Amelia…'

Amelia rolls her eyes and heads to the door.

Debbie watches Amelia crossing the room. She knows something is about to happen, something planned, something that's part of this entire ordeal, and she knows that when Amelia opens the door, everything's going to change. And any last semblance that this could be a normal desert jaunt will fall away.

Amelia opens the door.

Debbie looks at the ceiling, white tiles. And then she breathes and sits up as the light from the hallway spills into the room.

'What do you want?' Amelia asks the two men standing at the door.

One is the concierge, and the other, a security guard. Twenty stone of muscle with a gun, a huge fucking gun, right at his side.

'Yusef requests your presence in the main hall.'

'It's 2am…' Amelia points out weakly. Debbie can hear the tremor in her voice; she's clocked the gun.

'We're aware it's late, but the evening's entertainment is not over yet. Please come with me.'

Amelia looks to Debbie. Debbie takes her in, standing, in her fluffy pyjamas, her fleecy top featuring a penguin. Her eyes are wide, scared, childlike. Her hair is plaited in Pocahontas braids.

Debbie feels acute pity for her friend. Guilt. She wouldn't be here if Debbie hadn't convinced her to come. And now here they both are, about to be forced into something, something really, really bad.

'You need to come to the main hall now,' the security guard says, his voice low and gruff.

Debbie eyes him and his gun, and her eyes water, her heart rate quickening.

'Amelia, we have to go,' she says, getting out of bed and putting on her sliders.

Trance-like, Amelia dons her dressing gown. She's on autopilot, but Debbie can see her hands quivering, her body shaking.

Debbie tries to stay calm.

As long as she doesn't think too much or look at the gun, she can carry on pretending. She can carry on deluding herself that this is somehow normal and not absolutely fucking terrifying.

'This way,' the concierge says, and the girls follow him down the corridor, the security guard behind them.

CHAPTER NINETEEN

There's something inevitable about the feeling Debbie gets when she and Amelia are led into a large room, which has been covered in plastic sheeting.

It's all over the floor, even partway up the walls. It's like something from Dexter. Sitting in a semi-circle of ostentatious, golden throne-like seats, are the men from dinner, including Yusef. They eye the girls with dark, hungry eyes. They're dressed in black tie dinner wear, their finest suits. They look far smarter than they did at dinner. *This* is clearly the main event. Next to them are three spinning wheels like something from a game show, as well as a huge TV screen and a table heaped with objects, too far away to make out clearly, but which resemble either torture implements or sex toys.

Classical music is playing. It's soft and gentle, completely at odds with the horror of what is happening.

Half the girls from dinner are already in the hall. They sit in pairs on the floor, and worse, a few sit alone. Some are trembling, vividly trembling. A few stare at the ground, as though zoned out, disassociating with shock.

Debbie and Amelia are guided by the guards to a spot on the plastic-covered floor. They sit down. Amelia is shaking and Debbie is lightheaded. Her blood runs cold. It literally feels cold in her veins, a sensation she's never experienced before.

She and Amelia cling to each other, while the guard glare at them, before walking away.

More girls from dinner trickle in, in their pajamas and dressing gowns, also escorted by hotel staff and armed guards.

What is this? Debbie wonders.

Could this be a Hostel-type situation? Here, in the middle of nowhere, could she and Amelia be about to lose their lives, having unwittingly walked into the clutches of rich, powerful sadists?

Amelia vibrates with fear.

'What the fuck?' she whispers to Debbie, her eyes tortured and full of terror in a way Debbie has never seen before.

Debbie doesn't know what to say.

She feels responsible. She suggested this trip. She's the one who started talking to Yusef. She wanted to come to the desert.

Dotted around the room are security guards. Grizzled tanks of men, heavily armed.

The girls can't protest. They can't kick off. They can't run.

They're here now. In this room in the middle of nowhere. With strange, smirking men, and there is nothing they can do about it.

CHAPTER TWENTY

All the influencers invited to the mansion have now been plucked from their rooms and escorted to the main hall.

Some are crying. Some are shaking. One shouts out in protest, until a gun is pointed in her face, at which point she quickly quietens down. Goes quiet as a mouse.

A man steps forward. Nigel, from dinner. That boring dweeb who Debbie thought was benign. He's wearing a three-piece suit now with a flamboyant ruffle-necked shirt and a purple bowtie, and he has an evil smile on his face, a self-satisfied look that gives Debbie chills.

'Welcome, ladies,' he says, with an expansive gesture, encompassing the terrified young women before him.

'You're no doubt wondering what tonight's festivities entail. Well, tonight, we'll be playing a very special game. It's a game we've been looking forward to for a while now, and we're thrilled to finally be playing it with you.'

One of the girls cries, audibly. She weeps.

The men smirk. Excitement radiates off them.

'Tonight, one million dollars is up for grabs. Yes, you heard that right, ladies. One million dollars!'

Amelia grips Debbie's hand. Her palm is sweaty and slick.

'You could leave tonight with hundreds of thousands of dollars in your bank account. Life-changing amounts of money!'

Some of the men titter. This is spare change to them.

The words 'leave tonight' resonate in Debbie's brain, though. At least murder seems to be off the cards.

'Let me explain the rules of the game.'

Debbie looks to Amelia, whose eyes are filled with tears. She looks down at the floor.

'There are three rounds. And three wheels.'

Nigel walks towards the wheels and gestures at one of them.

'This wheel is for round one. It contains dares, each of which will earn you $30,000. Not a bad amount of money.'

More laughter.

'Accept the dare, complete it successfully, and the money will be instantly transferred to your PayPal or Venmo account by our resident accountant, Amir.'

Nigel gestures towards a diminutive-looking man sitting in front of a computer, nerdy in a v-neck. He gives a little wave, like this is all perfectly normal.

'You'll be able to see the transfer take place on the screen to my right.'

Nigel gestures towards the TV screen.

'Are you all following?'

None of the girls react.

'I'll take that as a yes, I guess. Wheel two also features dares, each of which is worth $60,000. Complete your dare, and the money will be deposited into your account.'

A tear rolls down Amelia's cheek.

'Wheel three, my favourite wheel.' Nigel laughs and then corrects himself. '*Everyone's* favourite wheel contains dares worth $100,000. Yes, you heard that right! One hundred thousand dollars! Complete your dare, and the money will be transferred straight to you. Just think of all the handbags you could buy!'

The men snigger.

'If you pass on a dare, you make nothing, and you miss your turn. But the more dares you complete, the more money you make. It's simple. The game ends when the money runs dry. There's a million dollars to play for tonight, ladies. A million dollars.'

Nigel smiles, satisfied with his gamemaster skills.

'She who dares, wins. Do you all understand?'

The girls are quiet, stunned. A few nod. A few tremble.

'If you want to play, remain sitting where you are, and we will commence the game shortly. If you don't wish to play, you can now leave. You will be escorted back to your room and driven back to your hotel. Those who stay and play the game will leave at midday tomorrow. You have five minutes to make your decision. Stay and play or leave now. The choice is yours.'

Debbie and Amelia look at each other.

Debbie has never seen Amelia look so shaken, so distressed.

'Let's go,' Amelia says, her voice tremulous.

She moves to get up, her legs shaking.

Debbie doesn't budge.

'Come on!' Amelia attempts to pull Debbie up, but she remains seated. 'Debbie!'

Debbie looks to the men, who are eyeing the girls, pointing, joking, laughing, watching them like they're zoo animals.

She thinks of the money at stake. Hundreds of thousands of dollars. That's *a lot* of money. She could buy a place, perhaps. It may not be much to this bunch of psychopaths, but such sums could make a huge difference to her life.

She's sick of living hand to mouth, worrying about money all the time, being in debt, having to reach out to her mother for loans, leaning on her. If she plays this game, she could be set up for a few years, maybe longer.

Debbie reasons that she can leave if it gets too much. She doesn't have to accept dares. If they're too crazy, she can sit them out. She just won't make money that way. But she'll be missing out on money she already doesn't have. So what's to lose? If she does complete the dares, then she stands to gain.

'Debbie, come on! What the fuck?'

Debbie looks up at Amelia. Amelia wouldn't understand, couldn't understand. Amelia is loved. She's supported. Her family cares. She has a home, security, compassion. She has a safety net. She doesn't need the money.

'I'm staying,' Debbie says.

Amelia shakes her head. She blinks. Tears fall down her cheeks like arrows.

'No, you're not.'

Amelia attempts to tug Debbie up, but Debbie jerks her hand away.

'Go, Amelia.'

'Debbie, please,' Amelia says, softer now, crying. 'Please don't do this, please.'

Debbie looks at the ground. Maybe on some level she knew something like this was going to happen here. Maybe on some level, she's ready.

'If you need money, I'll help you. Please, I'm begging you,' Amelia pleads. 'Let's go.'

'Ladies!' Nigel's voice booms. 'You have one more minute to decide what you're going to do. If you're leaving, leave now, before the games commence.'

'Debbie!' Amelia cries.

Debbie looks to the floor.

'Debbie!'

More crying.

'Debbie, don't do this. We can leave. Forget all about this. Go back to the hotel. This isn't safe, Debbie. These men are *dangerous*.'

Debbie keeps looking at the floor.

'Debbie, I'm BEGGING YOU.'

Debbie's eyes are fixed on the floor.

'Debbie…'

More crying, and then Amelia is gone.

CHAPTER TWENTY-ONE

Seven girls remain.

They're nervous, shaking, and they glance at each other with sad, scared eyes.

'Let the games commence!' Nigel booms, smiling like a Cheshire Cat.

The men pop bottles of champagne and fill their flutes.

Debbie's heart beats fast.

She looks towards the exit, manned by two guards, who glare at the girls.

She tries not to think about the look in Amelia's eyes and instead focuses on the money.

Nigel sips his champagne before booming into the microphone, 'Now who wants to go first?'

The girls glance at each other, but no one puts themself forward.

'Okay.' Nigel sighs. 'How about this?'

He points towards the girls. 'Eeny, meeny, miny, moe,' he says, tracing his finger around the group, 'catch a tiger by the toe; if it squeals, let it go: eeny, meeny, miny, moe.'

His finger lands on the woman Debbie saw at dinner who was wearing that gorgeous Prada dress. She's in a nightgown now. A cute, white one, with lace embroidery. Debbie thinks of the way she was laughing at dinner. She clearly hadn't cottoned on at that point that there was something not quite right about this place. She thought she was on a normal holiday. And now, she's cowering, terrified.

'Lydia, isn't it?' Nigel says.

The woman nods.

'Right, Lydia, how are you feeling tonight?'

Lydia doesn't respond. The men stare at her.

'Fabulous chat, Lydia. Well, let's spin the wheel of fortune, or misfortune in your case!'

All the men laugh.

Nigel spins the wheel. Lydia shakes.

The wheel slows to a halt.

Nigel reads the dare the wheel has landed on.

'Rock pelting! A nice little warm-up.'

The men titter, devouring hor d'oeuvres.

'Are you willing to have rocks thrown at you, Lydia? For thirty thousand dollars!'

Lydia starts to cry.

'Lydia, do you accept the challenge, or do you forfeit the dare?'

Lydia looks at the floor. Some of the men wander over to the table and pick up rocks, holding them, inspecting their weight, eager to get going.

'I need an answer, Lydia,' Nigel insists.

Debbie rolls her eyes. She can tell Nigel is loving this.

Lydia nods.

'Is that a yes, Lydia?'

'Yes,' Lydia replies, her tone flat.

More men grab rocks.

'Come on then. Come over here,' Nigel says.

Lydia gets up.

Nigel beckons her towards the men.

She stands before them, head bowed.

'Congratulations on accepting your challenge, Lydia! For $30,000, you will now be pelted with rocks!'

Lydia sobs.

She turns to the women, most of whom are crying too, wincing, unable to look.

'I'll do anything for my kids,' she says, as the first rock hits her hard on the neck.

CHAPTER TWENTY-TWO

'Debbie! What's your dare going to be?' Nigel jeers as he spins the wheel.

Debbie has watched three women be abused now, in a range of revolting, sickening ways, and she's zoning out. She tells herself she can sit the dares out, that she doesn't have to partake. But she's also shutting down, switching off, and wondering how much she can earn, how much she can take.

The wheel of misfortune spins before eventually drawing to a halt.

'To win $30,000, you, Debbie, have to be a dog.'

'What?' Debbie scoffs.

'Bark. Eat dog food. Act like a dog. Can you do that, Debbie?'

Debbie's palms bead with sweat.

Thirty thousand dollars...

'Okay,' Debbie replies.

'This should be good!' Nigel, the man who sat next to Debbie over dinner and pretended to be civilised, says.

Debbie gets up.

She walks over to the men. She tries not to look at them, but a few catch her eye. They're smirking, jeering, sipping champagne, and plucking hors d'oeuvres presented to them by passing waiters, who are circling around them, tending to their needs, dressed in full-length tuxedos.

Debbie gets on her knees.

'Woof then,' one of the men says.

'Woof,' Debbie says.

'Bark like you mean it. Like you're an actual dog,' the man spits, clearly unimpressed.

Debbie barks more aggressively, more roughly, channelling a canine. She feels wild, deranged, and degraded.

The men laugh and holler and whoop.

Debbie barks and barks, hoping this will satisfy them, that it will be over.

But then one of the men comes up to her. He's huge and old with a red, pocked face and a neck like a turkey.

'I am going to call you Fluffy,' he says in a thick German accent as he bends down to pat her on the head.

The man, Ulf Hoffman, is a dentist from Hamburg. He owns an exclusive practice where he handles complex, restorative maxillofacial dentistry. He's one of the most respected names in his field, nationally and internationally, and he regularly travels to feature as a key note speaker at dentistry conferences. He lives alone following a divorce five years ago from his wife, Helga. He owns five high-end properties across Germany and Switzerland. He plays golf whenever life affords him the opportunity, has no children, and he deeply, deeply despises women. And most men too, for that matter.

'How are you doing, my little Fluffy?'

Debbie can smell the man. He smells stale and sour, like body odour and dead skin.

He steps closer and reaches down to tickle Debbie's neck.

Debbie freezes.

Ulf turns and walks over to the table. He picks something up that Debbie can't quite make out.

As he comes back, she sees it. A leash.

Debbie's heart sinks as Ulf, smirking, leans down and clips a collar around her neck.

'Good Fluffy,' Ulf says, sneering down at her with his dark eyes and a flaccid face.

Debbie looks to the ground.

Ulf tugs at the lead.

Debbie tries to resist its pull, but the collar pulls at her neck.

She thinks of Angel, little Angel, and her eyes prick with tears.

'Come on, Fluffy.'

Ulf pulls harder on the lead. Debbie can no longer resist the tug of it.

She follows Ulf, walking on all fours in circles on the plastic floor as the men sip champagne and point and laugh.

Debbie tries not to look at them. She focuses on the floor. The clear plastic, crinkling under her hands and knees.

Finally, Ulf draws to a halt. Debbie's neck is raw from the collar. She doesn't know what to do with the quivering feeling in her heart.

'Bark for Daddy, Fluffy.'

Debbie looks up. Has she not been degraded enough already? All the men are staring at her.

The security guards with their guns are watching too. Even the waiters pause, holding their big silver plates of hors d'oeuvres still, paying attention.

Debbie wonders if she should bail, be done with this, forfeit the dare, but then she just barks.

She barks like an angry dog. She starts barking at this disgusting man, at all the men; she shows her teeth, snapping at this grotesque man's calloused feet. She barks like she's wild. She barks like she's been caged.

'Good girl, Fluffy!' Ulf says, and he hands her something. 'Have a treat.'

Ulf presents her with a bowl of dog food. A big bowl, a dog's bowl, full of glistening wet chunks of meat and jelly.

It reeks. Cheap, nasty dog food. Even the smell of it makes Debbie want to gag.

'Eat up, Fluffy.'

Debbie looks up at this man. This fat, repulsive, rich old man.

She looks into his dark, menacing, empty eyes, and she wonders what happened to him, where he came from, where it all went wrong.

'For thirty thousand dollars, eat your dinner, Fluffy,' Nigel interjects.

The men laugh.

Debbie looks at the dog bowl. What kind of meat is it? Beef? Pork? Chicken? A pulverized mix of all? Dog food is the cast offs, isn't it? The bits of meat that can't be sold to customers. The eyeballs and assholes and brains. Debbie tries not to think about that. She glances up at the man before her, eyes pleading, wanting him to take mercy. Hasn't she humiliated herself enough already?

But of course, he's not going to take mercy. He eyes her with a cool, angry stare.

'Eat your fucking dinner, you bitch,' Ulf says, and then he pushes Debbie's face into the bowl. The cool jelly squelches over her skin.

She opens her mouth and tries not to think about what she's doing as she takes a bite of the dog food. *It's just meat. Meat and jelly*, she tells herself. It's just meat. Her mouth is just a mouth. She just has to open her mouth, close it, swallow, and repeat, until the food is gone. As long as she doesn't think about it too much, it'll be okay.

But the dog food is revolting and Debbie can't stop herself from gagging, sputtering into the bowl as Ulf pushes her head down. He's not going to stop pushing her head into the bowl until it's all gone. So Debbie sputters, and eats, and tries to cast her mind elsewhere, to a tropical beach, a blue sky, a glittering sea, a breeze blowing through her hair. She keeps her mind there, on a beach. She pictures herself lounging on the sand, sailboats in the distance, the sound of children playing and laughing, the sound of joy, and she eats.

Finally, after what feels like forever, the food is gone.

Debbie feels sick, but she looks up at Ulf, hoping that's it. That's got to be it.

'Good, Fluffy. You're a good dog,' Ulf says,

patting Debbie's head once more.

Debbie wants to bite his hand off, tear flesh. Her skin prickles with disgust. This man is evil, sick.

The ka-ching sound of a closing cash register sounds, and Debbie looks up to see the funds being deposited into her bank account, live on screen.

She retreats to the spot she was sitting in before. She's nauseous. Bile rises in her throat. She swallows it down, but it keeps returning.

As Nigel spins the wheel for the next girl, Debbie turns her head and vomits on the floor.

CHAPTER TWENTY-THREE

Justin Twain lights a cigarette.

He doesn't often smoke. He reserves smoking as an occasional treat for after really good sex or at these events. His favourite time to smoke is this precise moment, mid-way through the competition, when the girls are writhing and crying on the floor. The weakest having quit during round one, with the most desperate remaining.

Sometimes the girls grow competitive at this stage. They unlock an animal instinct in themselves, and they switch off their humanity; they become something else. There are four girls still playing.

Justin takes a deep drag of his cigarette and eyes them. There's Lydia, the single mother, with the sweet Baby Spice sort of look. Then there's Svetlana, a high-end prostitute from St Petersburg, or was it Moscow? The girl's sexy as fuck and hard as nails. She's hired to keep things going. Her participation normalises proceedings for the other girls. She's beautiful and classy-looking, enviably attractive, and if a girl like her is willing to play a game like this, then maybe the other girls should too? Or at least that's the idea. And Svetlana cashes out from the dares too. She stands to gain as much money as anyone else by playing, on top of her fee to attend. She's also competitive, and that makes things interesting.

Then there's Tina. Looks barely eighteen and not someone Justin imagined would make it this far. She was sitting near him at dinner, talking about how she was studying at a talent school and wanted to be the next Adele. She was all wide, starry eyes. And yet here she is, degrading herself for money. She seems oddly tough now though, driven. Justin wonders whether her dinner persona was an act or if she's uncovering darker sides to herself in real time. It's funny what the desert and the allure of money can do to a person. He's seen stranger behaviour out here.

Then there's Debbie. Debbie, the influencer from Essex. Justin has browsed Debbie's Instagram page quite a few times over the past few months, and he has to admit she caught his eye. She's the real deal, as far as he can tell. Just the kind of girl he likes to play this game.

She's young, sexy, pretty, and somewhat interesting judging by the expression in her eyes in some of her pictures. She doesn't look totally vapid, and she sometimes writes thoughtful captions accompanying her pictures, which betray a certain intelligence. From having dug around on her page, Justin notes she went to Edinburgh University years ago, too. She has potential, and yet she's here. Most of the nice girls, girls like her friend Amelia, leave. The ones who stay tend to have something wrong with them. A hurt, a pain, a trauma, a self-destructive streak. Debbie was probably abused at some point. Probably unloved.

Justin noticed that there were no photos of her on her Instagram page with her family. And she doesn't smile much in her pictures either. In the rare ones where she is smiling, it's a beautiful smile. One of those cute wide ones, with dimples. The kind of smile that lights up a person's whole face. Justin wonders what he could do to take that smile away.

What could he do to Debbie? How far could he push her? She's been trembling ever since the game began. She's deeply shaken, and Justin can tell she's the kind of girl who'll get PTSD from something like this. Who'll have flashbacks for years. She's the kind of girl he could really make an impression on. There's nothing Justin likes more than traumatising a young woman and then watching her crumble on Instagram afterwards. There's nothing quite like it. That's the great thing about Instagram girls. You can witness the aftermath online. You don't get that with regular whores. Sometimes he can see in the girls' pictures that the light's gone out in their eyes. They smile and pose; they flaunt handbags and nice clothes, but they're different. And that makes Justin feel powerful. Strangely, it makes him feel less alone.

Justin has been coming to these parties for three years now. Three or four times a year, whenever they're on. He never misses them. They're usually here, in this mansion, but there's a site near Amsterdam too. Another in LA. The men in attendance have a WhatsApp group chat, innocuously titled 'Socialising'.

In this chat, they discuss upcoming events, keeping everything as normal-sounding as possible. The events are 'parties'; the girls they want to abuse are 'guests'. The men browse Instagram, looking for good guests. Pretty girls that take their fancy.

Suitable guests are girls who don't look like they have much in the way of support. Vulnerable girls. Girls without close families. Without too many friends. Girls the men sense need something: money, validation, love. They screenshot their pictures and share their profiles to the group chat, discuss them, weigh up their suitability, and if the group greenlights them, then Yusef reaches out. He gives them the whole spiel about coming to review the hotel, dazzling them with its ultra-luxurious Instagram page. Nine times out of ten, they don't reply, sensing something's not quite right. Probably even more often than that. Sometimes they reply initially and then realise something's up and disappear. But sometimes, they fall right into the trap, just like Debbie did.

When the group first started holding these competitions, they used prostitutes as participants. But a lot of them had done degrading stuff before for money, and they just weren't scared enough. They didn't tremble. They didn't cry. Not much anyway. That's when the men had the idea to recruit regular women, and they started using Instagram like an online shop. And that's when the parties really became fun.

Justin takes a drag of his cigarette and watches as Lydia weeps while being abused.

He feels completely relaxed.

Here, at this mansion, he gets to unmask, unwind.

These events are an oasis of calm for him, a reprieve in his calendar where he gets to be himself. He doesn't have to pretend anymore. Not one bit.

He's around other people just like him, doing bad things, unleashing their darkness with no shame. They get to be awful together, openly. It's freeing. So fucking freeing.

So much of Justin's life is spent pretending.

He has to pretend to be a loving husband, a loving dad. A normal person with empathy and moral standards. He spends most of his time at the office simply to avoid the drain of being at home, where e has to constantly pretend to care about meaningless shit.

And it helps that there are bad people in his industry. Callousness pays in the record business in a way it doesn't exactly tend to in family life. Being dog-eat-dog gets you places.

But there's nowhere quite like here. This house is in the middle of nowhere. A lawless place where none of these girls' screams would be heard. Where none of them could be traced if they went missing. They could be disappeared here unbelievably easily. And they know it. The fear emanates off them, the horror in their eyes, their desperation and terror; it's a shot in the arm to Justin. It satisfies him in a way he can hardly put into words. It's better than sexual satisfaction. It's like an orgasm for his whole psyche. A deep release.

This time next weekend, Justin will be in Durham with his wife, having visited his son, Matthew, at university. They'll be sleeping in a nice bed in the bed and breakfast they always stay at. The one with shabby chic furniture and quirky pictures on the walls. And in the morning, they'll get dressed for a hike across the Pennine Way with Matthew. They'll take pictures on the moors before going for a Sunday roast, where they'll talk encouragingly about Matthew's future—his plans to become a doctor, his hopes and dreams—and Matthew will return to his university dorm feeling loved and supported. And Justin's wife will feel content and peaceful as they drive back to London, the sun setting, the sky a bluish hue.

But for now, Justin has someone he needs to hurt. He stubs out his cigarette, rubs the Freemason pendant dangling around his neck—a cherished necklace that belonged to his grandfather—for luck, and walks over to the girls.

CHAPTER TWENTY-FOUR

It's Debbie's turn.

'And what has the wheel got in store for you, Debbie?' Nigel booms, still in full compere mode.

His eyes are glittering. He can't stop smiling. Debbie imagines him, back home, in whatever finance job he has, sitting behind his computer all day, a non-entity, waiting to do this, eager for this moment. It's the highlight of his year no doubt.

He spins the wheel, and there's silence in the room as it whirls, everyone watching. Finally, the wheel lands on a dare.

'Take a horse whip! Will you, Debbie, for sixty thousand dollars, be whipped? Now this isn't just with a regular whip, the kind you get from Ann Summers during your *Fifty Shades of Grey* phase.'

The men titter.

'This is with a horse whip. Have you seen one of those before, Debbie?'

One of the men from dinner – the one who was staring at her and wearing that strange necklace – steps forward. His eyes are dark and intense, and he looks at Debbie in a way she hasn't been looked at before. She's been desired by men, plenty of times. She's seen desire cloud their eyes like smoke. She's been glared at by men too, regarded with bitter, angry eyes following a rejection, or simply glared at by men who don't much like women. But the way Justin is looking at her is different. It's a hungry stare, but it's not lustful. It's piercing but not admiring. Something about the intensity of his gaze unnerves Debbie more than the sight of the whip he picks up from the table.

It's a long black whip. A riding whip, made from thick black leather. Nigel was right. This isn't the kind of whip you'd get from Ann Summers; it's something else entirely.

This is the sort of whip used to torture a person.

The sort of whip that could lacerate. Could it even kill?

But $60,000. That's a lot of money. Debbie doesn't know the exchange rate off the top of her head, but it must be around £50,000. That's more than Debbie makes in a year. A lot more. She could pay for her rent for years with that.

Debbie wouldn't have to ask her mum for money anymore. She wouldn't have to make those embarrassing calls where she swallows her pride, asks for cash, and cringes as she cements her mother's intrinsic view that she's a failure, good for nothing, a fool. Fifty thousand pounds would grant her some independence. She could do things, be free.

Getting whipped will be painful, sure. It will be horrific. But some people are into stuff like this. Some people do this sort of thing for fun. Debbie doesn't know much about BDSM. She's had a few guys choke her and slap her about a bit in bed, but nothing too kinky. But she knows there are sites that cater to people into this kind of thing. There are communities dedicated to such fetishes. There are probably people who do this kind of thing on a Friday night. For free.

Debbie sighs.

She doesn't want to be whipped by this creepy man with his dark eyes, and every cell in her body wants nothing to do with the situation, but she finds she can't turn the dare down. She can't quite do it.

She wants the money. Needs the money.

'Do you accept the dare, Debbie? Will you allow Justin to whip you?' Nigel presses.

'Yes,' Debbie says, under her breath.

She sees the man – Justin – smile, his grip on the whip tightening, and her stomach squirms.

'What was that, Debbie?'

'I accept the dare,' Debbie says, louder, trying not to glare at Nigel.

She doesn't want to give in to the campness of his gamemaster act. The whole thing is such a sick farce. She wonders how far these men have travelled to be here. How much they've spent on this. Debbie doesn't want to think about it.

Waiters present fresh plates of hors d'oeuvres to the men as they sit sultan-like on their thrones. Yusef plucks one from a plate and smiles charmingly at the waiter, like he's at a high-end restaurant. Debbie can't make out the hors d'oeuvres from where she's sitting, but she sees flashes of rainbow-coloured food, artful creations. They're no doubt lovely.

'Step forward, please, Debbie,' Nigel says.

Debbie gets up from the ground.

She tries not to look at Justin, who she can feel is staring at her.

She doesn't want to see his dark, eager eyes.

She approaches.

She's still wearing her pajamas. They smell of vomit and dog food and sweat. She feels grotesque. She can feel all the men looking at her, eyeing her like they're spectating a bull fight.

'Take your top off,' Justin says.

'What?'

'I said take your top off.'

'But…'

Debbie didn't sign up for this. She's wearing nothing underneath.

'You heard me. I'm not whipping you through your clothes.'

The men laugh.

Debbie looks to Nigel, as though expecting him to mediate. As though he might show mercy.

'You heard him,' Nigel comments.

Debbie narrows her eyes and looks to the ground as she unbuttons her top. She can't look at anyone, and her hands shake as she moves from button to button, her fingers clammy and unsteady.

She hears the pop of a champagne cork.

'Get on with it!' One of the men hollers.

She pictures the man, swigging from his champagne, maybe popping a new bottle open.

She refuses to look up as she unbuttons each button, getting to the final one. She takes her top off, still looking at the ground as she tosses it to the side.

It's just a body. It's just skin. It's just a chest, Debbie tells herself as the men holler and jeer. *It's just flesh.*

If she allows herself to think of her body as something personal, something special, something sacred, something that matters, she'll cry. So, she doesn't.

'Good,' she hears Justin say. 'Now get on the ground.'

She glances at him. His face is snarling, venomous.

He's the sort of man who might have been attractive at one point.

He's tall, imposing. 6'3" perhaps. He has reasonable features, although age has rendered them worn and unremarkable. His dark eyes are probably eyes that some women have gazed into. There are women out there who probably found his eyes captivating, mysterious, challenging even. Perhaps they were drawn to that darkness, wanting to save him, help him.

But a man like him can't be saved. A man like him is dark by nature. A man like him feeds his darkness.

Debbie shrinks to the ground.

'Get on all fours,' Justin insists.

Debbie gets on all fours.

'Very nice,' Justin says.

His voice is lusty, and Debbie can hear how much he's getting off on this already.

Debbie looks to the ground, not wanting to engage with Justin, but in her peripheral vision, she sees him crack the whip.

It makes a whooshing, high-pitched noise as it slices the air. Debbie winces from the noise alone, and she has a horrible feeling that she's making a big mistake. She braces herself, but the blow doesn't come.

She considers backing down, forfeiting her dare, when Justin cracks the whip again, and this time it lands on her back, slashing against her, causing a blast of pain so severe she can't even cry out. She just grits her teeth, her eyes watering, and tries not to faint.

Justin cracks the whip again. It crashes against her. The pain is unbearable. Justin cracks the whip again. And again. And Debbie isn't sure if she'll live. This is what being murdered must feel like. Visualising beaches won't save her this time. This is something else.

Debbie cries, weeps. Tears leak from her eyes, and she can hardly stay on all fours.

The pain is excruciating, off the scale. The men are laughing and jeering, hollering. They're loving it.

Debbie thinks of home, her mother, Angel.

She wants to go home.

'Stop. Stop,' she cries out.

The whip is slick now. Her back is wet.

Blood is seeping from her sides, onto the plastic. Drop. Drop. Drop.

Debbie's legs give way.

She collapses to the plastic, foetal-like.

'Have that, bitch. Have that, you dirty fucking whore,' Debbie can hear Justin saying as the whip cracks through the air again, lacerating her bloody flesh.

'Please stop,' she begs.

Debbie looks up at Justin. His features are contorted. He wears an evil, rage-twisted sneer. His teeth are bared, and his eyes are black. He looks like something from a horror film. He looks like a demon.

Debbie has never seen someone look so inhuman, so utterly grotesque. She tries to blink the image away. She wishes she hadn't seen it. She knows she'll be haunted by it. He looks like something that's risen from hell.

'Stop. Stop,' she urges, looking at the floor, her vision blurring.

Justin cracks the whip again.

'That's it,' Nigel says. 'You're going to kill her.'

Justin groans.

'One more?'

'Fine.'

And then the whip cracks through the air and lands hard on Debbie's flesh, and she screams.

And it's finally over.

Distantly, she hears the 'ka-ching' sound.

'Congratulations, Debbie! Sixty thousand dollars has been transferred to your account. We hope you enjoy your prize.'

Debbie looks up.

She sees on screen the money landing in her PayPal account. And she hates the fact that part of her, in spite of being blood-drenched, tear-drenched, and fearing for her life, feels glad.

CHAPTER TWENTY-FIVE

Debbie is lightheaded as the game continues.

The plastic she sits on is bloody. She thinks of how she must look. A girl sitting in a pool of blood.

The men sipping their champagne are no doubt relishing the sight.

Her wounds sting, and pain ripples through her in waves. Reverberations from Justin.

She looks over at him. He's sitting on his throne. His dinner suit is blood-spattered. He looks dazed, like his thoughts are somewhere else. He seems completely relaxed. Debbie looks away.

Lydia is completing her dare. She's bound in leathers, a bondage outfit like nothing Debbie has seen before. It isn't sexy; it's frightening. Straps of leather, studs, spikes, and a leather balaclava with no eye holes render her nothing more than a piece of leather-bound flesh. A strange-looking object.

Several men take turns with her, throwing her around.

Debbie tries not to look. She tries to tune it out.

She tries to focus on the music. What is it? Bach? Schubert?

She's never listened to classical music much before, and she doubts she ever will after tonight. But it's better to focus on the scraps of melody than the grunts and groans and cheers and jeers from the men.

She rests her eyes on a crinkle in the plastic. How much has she made so far?

Being a dog got her $30,000; the whipping was for $60,000. So that's $90,000, around £70,000. It's so much money to Debbie. She wants to leave. She knows she should. She should forfeit her next dare.

She's been hurt enough, abused enough. Her heart is aching, and her back is throbbing. She knows it will probably never be the same after this.

What's it going to look like? Will she have permanent scars? There are products that are meant to reduce scarring, like Bio-Oil. Could Debbie slather herself with Bio-Oil every day and fade the scars? Or will the scarring be too severe? Horsewhip lashings probably aren't the kind of injury Bio-Oil is usually used on.

Debbie's thoughts are interrupted by the sound of a muffled scream.

One of the men is inserting a sex toy into Lydia.

Debbie looks away, revolted. This is too much. And yet strangely, she feels hollow.

Is this trauma? Shock? She feels shut down.

Lydia's muffled screams continue, and Debbie just stares at the crinkled plastic, waiting for her turn in the game, wondering if she'll be able to take the dare.

Eventually, the men tire of Lydia, and she's tossed away.

The money is transferred into her bank account. She returns to the plastic, where she takes off her leathers.

Debbie's turn arrives, and Nigel spins the wheel, gleeful as ever.

'For $60,000, you, Debbie, will allow Svetlana to use these toys on you.'

A range of sex toys are presented. They, like the whip, are not the kind of thing you'd find in Ann Summers. They look painful, terrifying, surgical.

Debbie doesn't want Svetlana to touch her with such odd contraptions.

She's never even been with a girl. Not that you could really call what Nigel is proposing as "being with" someone.

Lydia is sitting not far from Debbie, and she's crying and trembling from what she went through. The men didn't exactly take it easy on her.

And Debbie's still bleeding from Justin. She feels weak and jelly- like. She doesn't want to be poked and probed and hurt anymore. She wants to leave. She wants to go home. She wants to put all this behind her.

But if she leaves, then that's it. She'll have £70,000, or whatever it is. A good amount of money. But not £130,000. Not that. She might even be able to buy a home with £130,000. She's seen cheap places online. Flats at auction.

Perhaps she could get one. She thinks of Amelia, with her lovely flat, paid for by her dad, which she's furnished and personalised and made cute. She's painted the walls and decorated everything just the way she likes it. Debbie's never been able to do that. She can't even put a picture up without running it past her landlord.

Debbie looks to Svetlana, who eyes her with a cool, level stare. Svetlana doesn't look perturbed. She doesn't even look afraid. She just looks blank.

'Debbie, do you wish to accept your dare or forfeit it?'

Debbie looks at one of the sex toys. It looks gynaecological. A weird surgical-like contraption.

'It'll be okay,' Svetlana says, softly, just loud enough to carry over the music.

Debbie looks to her; her cool blue eyes soften a little. She's undeniably beautiful, and that pink streak in her hair adds character. Debbie imagines what she might be like normally, back home. A fun times girl, smiling in sunglasses with her friends. And yet here they both are. Debbie thinks of the money. And she decides, stomach lurching, to do it.

'Okay,' she says. 'I accept the dare.'

CHAPTER TWENTY-SIX

Debbie aches after her ordeal with Svetlana, but in a strange way, she has shut down, switched off.

She's almost getting used to these men, with their sick dares and their twisted laughter. Almost. The things she's doing are depraved, but as long as she doesn't think too much, she can get through it. She can line her bank account, handsomely. As long as she stays focused on that, she'll be okay. Or at least that's what she tells herself as she gears up for her next turn.

For another sixty thousand dollars, Debbie's has to have sex with a man while he carves his name into her flesh.

The man's name is Stephen, apparently.

He's tall and dark, but not exactly handsome. He's in his late fifties, maybe early sixties, and he has strange features, almost girlish. Long lashes and red lips on a wrinkled face with a greying hairline.

Debbie's on top of him, trying to ignore his smiling face.

He's hard and massive, and he fills her. His cock is thicker than most men she's been with. It's the kind of cock that overpowers you and doesn't work for tender sex.

It feels strangely good, and Debbie hates herself for that.

Here she is, fucking a creep in the worst circumstances imaginable, and her body is betraying her. She feels strangely aroused, like her desire is an entity beyond her morals, her rationality, and her tastes.

The man reaches for a knife at his side, which he's so far been ignoring.

It's not a big knife, to Debbie's relief. More like a pen knife.

He takes it and brings it to her chest.

'Stay still a minute,' he says.

And then he starts cutting into her.

Debbie winces, flinching as the blade pierces her flesh.

'Stay still,' Stephen hisses.

Debbie wants to pull back and recoil, but she can't. She wants the money. So she grits her teeth ad braces herself as Stephen carves.

S....T....E...

The pain is sharp and raw, but the letters Stephen is carving aren't too deep, and Debbie is grateful for that.

Stephen could have cut harder. He could have lacerated her. He could have scarred her for life, branded her forever. But he hasn't.

No doubt some of the men watching are disappointed.

Debbie wonders why Stephen didn't cut deeper. Maybe he doesn't want her to be permanently scarred.

Maybe Stephen is his real name, and he doesn't want to be linked to this event if it ever came to light.

If somehow these parties were ever investigated. Debbie reasons that must be the explanation.

Men like this wouldn't be merciful just for the sake of it.

Something happens as Stephen finishes carving his name. Something happens to Debbie.

She adjusts to the pain and feels a strange feeling, a dark thrill, as she looks down at this man's name on her body. She is not Debbie anymore.

She is something else.

She is Stephen, an extension of him. A part of her she hasn't met before finds she enjoys the detachment, the distance, and the feeling of being owned, branded, dominated.

A drop of blood trickles down her chest from the carved 'T'.

Debbie hates herself for the excitement her body feels. What kind of freak gets off on this? What's wrong with her?

Stephen flips her over. He pushes into her and his hand grips her throat, and Debbie finds herself gasping, moaning. The men cheer, and Stephen grins. Debbie hates herself, as pleasure ripples through her, obliterating her mind.

CHAPTER TWENTY-SEVEN

By the time Nigel spins the third wheel, Debbie is no longer scared. She isn't excited exactly, but she's intrigued. A darkness has seeped into her, and she's watching, waiting.

One of the tux-clad waiters who was serving hor d'oeuvres to the men, is now circling the girls, presenting a silver dish with freshly cut lines of white powder on it, along with silver tubes for snorting.

Debbie has consumed three lines of the powder already.

She doesn't know exactly what it is. The waiter has ignored her questions when asked, as though he didn't understand her. But she snorted the drugs anyway.

She suspects what she's consuming is cocaine. She's had coke a few times, at various parties. She's never been particularly into it, and she's never bought it herself. She's just accepted the odd line here and there. But Debbie recognises the alert feeling she's getting, the confidence, the sense of focus, the recklessness. She doesn't feel sad anymore. She doesn't even feel ashamed. It's good cocaine.

By Debbie's calculations, she's made around

£150,000 by this point, and she's hungry for more.

Wheel two is taken away, leaving wheel three. The big money wheel.

Nigel spins it. Lydia is up first.

'For one hundred thousand dollars, you have to give up your nipple.'

'Excuse me?' Lydia replies.

'Justin wants your nipple. For one hundred thousand dollars, will you allow Justin to have it?'

'What do you mean?'

Justin picks up a knife from the table and does a cutting motion over his chest.

'Fuck that!' Lydia exclaims. 'Fuck that! No fucking way.'

'You forfeit your dare?'

'Yes, I forfeit it. I want to leave. Right now.'

Nigel looks over to the guards.

'Please escort Lydia back to her room.'

The guards cross the hall. Lydia gets up. There's a haunted, rattled look in her eyes that Debbie doesn't want to engage with. Lydia has refused the drugs as far as Debbie is aware. She's scared and overwhelmed, traumatised, her feelings not blunted or warped.

She's been pelted with rocks, dressed in bondage gear and passed around like a piece of meat, and at one point, a while ago, her hair was hacked off, and now it's sticking out of her head in uneven clumps.

She's a far cry from the care-free girl she was at dinner, drinking champagne in her Prada dress, laughing, happy.

She tumbles as she tries to stand. She's shaking,

either from fear or pain; Debbie isn't sure.

The guards lift her to her feet and pull her away.

'Bunch of freaks,' Lydia shouts out as she walks away. She turns to the men, who are still supping on champagne, watching her with dark smiles.

'You bunch of sadistic fucks. Fucking psychos,' Lydia spits.

Debbie is surprised. Lydia has been quiet all night. Scared and desperate. And now here she is, spitting venom at these frightening men.

Nigel makes a slight motion with his hand, just a subtle flick of his fingers, almost imperceptible, but one of the guards registers it, and he whacks Lydia around the head with his gun.

She tumbles to the ground and starts sobbing.

The guard picks her up and she cries as she leaves the room.

'Does anyone else want to accept Lydia's dare? For one hundred thousand dollars, will you give up a nipple?'

Debbie looks to the ground.

She's unlocked darkness in herself tonight, that's for sure, but she isn't doing that. She wants to keep her nipples. One hundred thousand dollars is not a sum worth trading one for, she finds.

Only Debbie, Svetlana, and the young-looking girl from dinner, Tina, are left. And none of them will accept the dare.

Debbie wonders if she should leave.

Extreme BDSM is one thing, but mutilation? That's too much.

She should have known these men wouldn't give

away a hundred grand for nothing.

A waiter approaches again. He presents her with another line.

Debbie accepts it, hoovering up the powder.

She expected cocaine like before, but as the drug hits the back of her nasal passage and slides down her throat, she knows instantly that cocaine is not what she has taken.

It tastes different. It feels different.

The room starts to blur and spin, and Debbie feels trippy and fragmented. What is this? Everything starts blurring and merging. Sounds blend into one another. The classical music, the men's laughter and jeers, and Nigel's booming voice all merge together into a strange, warped symphony. A cacophony. A nightmarish sound. Debbie brings her hands to her ears, tries to get it to stop, but it won't go away. The room distorts too, like an oil painting, bleeding, its colours running and merging.

'What... was... that?' Debbie asks the waiter, or at least thinks she asks. He doesn't turn to her. He doesn't respond, and Debbie can't quite make out the sound of her own voice. Is she speaking? She tries to speak again, but something warbled comes out.

What's happening to her?

Fuck, Debbie thinks. *Fuck*.

Debbie doesn't know what's going on.

Time and space blur like her surroundings.

She hears screams, the wheel, and the ka-ching sound. Over and over. Along with sounds that don't feel quite real. That don't make sense.

She hears Amelia's voice – an auditory

141

hallucination. *Leave, Debbie. Come on, Debbie. Let's go.*

She hears jackals from the desert. She hears car engines and girls crying.

She doesn't know what's real anymore or what's imagined.

Her thoughts are blurring. She doesn't even know where she is anymore. What she's doing.

Nigel's saying something.

'Congratulations, Debbie. For one hundred thousand dollars, you will stab Tina.'

Another hallucination, Debbie tells herself.

Another trip.

And then she looks down, and in her hand, there's a knife, but it blurs, like watery paint, and dissolves to nothing.

CHAPTER TWENTY-EIGHT

When Debbie wakes up the next day, there's a brief moment when her hotel room is full of bright light – a moment of blankness – before reality descends like a bad dream.

There are deep wounds on her back, and they sting. Her muscles ache. Every part of her aches, including her head, which throbs. The feeling isn't like a hangover exactly. It's worse. It's pounding, acute.

The room spins slightly, like Debbie's still high.

Debbie thinks of the waiters with their lines of coke. She thinks of the third wheel, the jeering men.

The last dare she remembers doing is the one with Stephen, as he carved his name into her chest. She remembers Lydia leaving, hurling insults at the men and getting whacked around the head with a gun.

And then more drugs came, and she got high. Really high.

And then it's blank.

She took something else, something that wasn't coke; she vaguely remembers that. But that's where her memories end.

Debbie has no idea what she was given or what happened next.

Debbie's heart starts beating faster and her palms grow clammy. Fuck. Another panic attack is coming.

Debbie gets out of bed. She paces the room.

She opens a window, wanting fresh air, but the air outside is stifling and hot. Debbie pulls the window shut.

She walks to the bathroom and turns on the cold tap. Lowering her head to the sink, she drinks from it. Just for something to do. But the panic won't go. The throbbing, whirling feeling in her head won't quite go either.

Debbie crouches by the toilet bowl and sticks her fingers down her throat. She starts to gag, but nothing comes up. Just a few drips of bile.

She slumps onto the floor.

Vomiting wouldn't make last night go away. It's not like it can take away the after-effects of the drugs already coursing through her bloodstream. It's not like vomiting will bring back the memories of what happened after Lydia left.

And anyway, does Debbie really want to know what happened after that?

Perhaps it's merciful that she can't remember. Why would she want to remember?

Ignorance is bliss.

Suddenly, Debbie is hit with a terrifying thought. What if the men didn't transfer all the money she earned? What if the whole thing was theatre? An elaborate con?

Debbie wouldn't put it past those men. She wouldn't put anything past them.

She goes back to the bedroom and finds her phone. She sits on the bed and goes onto PayPal, typing in her password, barely breathing.

Please be there. Please be there, Debbie urges the money.

And then her account page is revealed: £244,000.

Debbie's hands start to shake.

That's a lot of money. An unbelievable amount. She's never had money like that.

She decides to transfer it out of her PayPal and into her bank account.

The creeps here know her PayPal details, and she doesn't want to risk getting hacked and having the money somehow taken away. This money is hers now. She earned it.

She fiddles about for a bit, and then the transfer goes through. And there it is: £244,000, sitting in her bank account.

A life-changing amount of money. A dizzying amount.

Debbie gets up.

She feels disoriented, charged, and adrenal, and yet her head is throbbing and her body aches. Her palms are clammy, beading with sweat. She's still scared, unnerved.

She could get murdered out here, and she'd never get to spend a penny. She wouldn't put it past those men to give her a bunch of cash, make her think her life is about to change, only to fucking kill her.

That's exactly the kind of thing they'd do. A final nasty little trick.

Debbie wishes Amelia were here. She wants to feel normal. She wants someone here who's normal.

A link to regular life. But Amelia is long gone. Her suitcase is nowhere to be seen. She'll probably be on the next flight back to London.

Debbie goes onto WhatsApp to message her and finds she's been blocked. Her profile picture, which was a shot of her smiling under a tree at her cousin's wedding, is now blank. Gone.

Debbie's stomach lurches.

She's been friends with Amelia for ten years, since school. And now they're over? Is that it?

She thinks of the look in Amelia's eyes as she urged her to leave. Amelia was desperate for her to get out of there. She understood the men were dangerous. Debbie should have realised what was at stake and that Amelia would probably not want

146

to know her if she went through with the twisted game being proposed. Debbie wonders if she'd take what she did back, forfeit the money for Amelia's friendship. And she decides that no, she probably wouldn't. It's not like they were ever really that close anyway.

Debbie checks the time on her phone. It's 11am.

She remembers something someone said during the game about the girls getting to leave at midday today. Debbie can't miss that. She has to get out of this place, she knows that much.

She goes to the bathroom to shower.

At some point last night, she put on her pajama top. She takes it off. The name 'Stephen' is etched onto her skin. She traces her fingertips over it, cringing at the memory of being with him. What happened to her in that moment? The letters are crusted over already. They'll heal and be gone soon. At least that's something.

But then Debbie checks the wounds on her back in the mirror - the lashings from Justin. She braces herself and freezes at her reflection. Her skin has been decimated, a crisscross of bloody lashings, like something from an extreme horror film. It's grotesque.

'No.'

She looks away. She can't believe how bad it is. She looks back, terrified.

The cuts are deep, visceral, horrifying.

'No. No, no, no.'

Debbie sinks to the bathroom floor, shaking, crying, unable to believe what she's done.

'No. No...'

After a while, numbness sets in. Debbie stares into space.

She's got a ton of money in her account, a life-changing amount. Her back has been decimated, her head is full of horrors, and her soul is on the floor, but she won't have to work for a while. She can recuperate for a bit, at least.

Eventually, Debbie gets up from the floor and decides to get dressed.

She knows that whatever she wears is going to end up bloody.

She didn't pack a 'post-abuse outfit' when she was preparing for this getaway. The most casual thing she has is a Moncler tracksuit, which cost nearly £400.

Debbie needs plasters. She needs bandages. But to get some, she'd have to speak to one of the hotel staff, and she doesn't want to do that. She doesn't want to do that at all.

So she puts sheets of toilet roll on her back. It sticks to the open wounds. Delicately, she puts on a T-shirt and then the tracksuit.

Even if the tracksuit does get blood on it, she can always buy a new one with the funds lining her bank account.

Debbie feels other, removed from herself as she gathers her things, her makeup, still on the dressing table from last night, her toiletries, her perfume. Her stuff feels like it belongs to a stranger. A different girl. The yesterday version of herself, who she'll never be again.

Debbie packs everything and heads down to reception. The men last night said something about the girls getting driven back at midday. It's close to midday now. Debbie puts on her shades, not caring if it's weird to wear them indoors. At this point, it really doesn't matter.

Svetlana is standing in the lobby with her suitcase, texting.

She's got a black eye and a split lip.

Her whole face is swollen. She glances at Debbie as she approaches. Debbie can barely look at her, after what went on between them last night.

'The drivers are nearly ready,' Svetlana says, her tone light and casual.

Debbie nods, noting that Svetlana doesn't seem ashamed or embarrassed. She doesn't seem traumatised, or like she's carrying any of the turbulence Debbie is feeling. She did things to Debbie last night that no one has ever done to her, but Svetlana doesn't seem in the least bit self-conscious.

Instead, she just looks bored and blank. Like she's waiting in a hotel reception on any other day.

Aside from her injuries, everything else about her is immaculate. She's dressed nicely in fitted jeans and a crewneck sweater, with a Hermès scarf tied neatly around her neck and a Ted Baker suitcase by her feet.

Her impeccable outfit makes her wounds look even more out of place, even more bizarre.

Debbie doesn't know what to do or what to say. This is the same girl who took her and Amelia's picture when they were quad biking, who was laughing and joking just yesterday, who seemed carefree and fun. And now here she is, beaten and abused and strangely casual.

Debbie gets her phone from her bag and stares at it as though Svetlana isn't there.

What do you do when you've seen someone be degraded in the worst possible ways? You can't make chit-chat. You can't talk about the weather.

Debbie looks down at her phone. She clicks through her gallery for something to do. She takes in the shots of her and Amelia quad biking, looking normal. Will she ever feel that way again?

Sensing movement, Debbie glances up and sees Lydia, hobbling across the lobby. She's swamped in a hoodie. It's pulled up over her head, hiding her hacked-off hair. She looks awful; her face is blotchy, and her eyes are swollen from crying. She glances at Debbie, and her expression is haunted, lost. Debbie shudders and looks away. She looks back down to her phone.

Lydia passes, and when Debbie looks back up, she sees she's sitting on the other side of the lobby, staring into space, detached and weirdly still. She looks possessed.

Debbie's heartrate quickens. She needs to get out of here.

She glances around. Where's Tina?

She must not have come down yet.

Debbie looks back at her phone and scrolls through her gallery, not taking anything in. Her head is spinning. This whole thing is so strange.

Debbie can feel another panic attack coming on. She reminds herself to breathe.

Just breathe.

'My first time was bad too,' Svetlana comments.

Debbie looks up.

'What?'

'My first time here was bad, but I just switch off now. What happens here stays here. I just detach.'

Debbie's chest tightens.

She doesn't want to speak to Svetlana. She just wants to get out of here. She can't believe

Svetlana has been here more than once. What's wrong with her?

'This is a crazy house, and crazy things happen,' Svetlana continues. 'But you have to move on and live your life. You weren't in control of yourself last night. They drugged you. What happened was bad, really bad…'

Svetlana's voice cracks up. She looks to the ground. Debbie eyes her. What's she talking about?

'But it wasn't you. You didn't know what you were doing. It wasn't your fault. It was theirs.'

Debbie's heart races.

What happened last night?

'I think my driver's outside,' Debbie says. 'I have to go.'

It's a lie, and both of them know it.

Debbie doesn't look at Svetlana again, or Lydia, as she heads outside, pulling her suitcase behind her.

The hot desert air hits her in the face like a hair dryer. But she stands against the mansion wall, breathes, tries to steady herself. She brings her hand to her chest, trying to quell her quickening heart.

It's a bright day. Too bright. Debbie takes in the manicured gardens, the palm trees, and the Maseratis and Ferraris still in the car park. Some have gone, but most of them are still there.

What are the men doing now? Debbie wonders. She pictures them in the hotel spa, relaxing, pleased with themselves, while Debbie stands here feeling like she might throw up. Wondering bleakly what exactly she did last night, and whether her life is ever going to be the same again.

Debbie spots movement in the car park. Two of the hotel concierges are carrying something to one of the cars. A large bag. Black and lumpy, long. It looks almost like a body bag. *No.* Debbie laughs to herself.

Of course not. It must be luggage.

The men load the bag into the back of a car and slam the doors.

It was luggage, Debbie tells herself. *Luggage*, she insists, as the men get into the car and drive away.

CHAPTER TWENTY-NINE

Debbie feels panic cascade through her as she is driven back to the city. It rises and falls like the desert dunes.

Her driver is a different one from yesterday, thankfully, and he seems completely disinterested in Debbie, which comes as a relief.

Looking blankly out of the window, Debbie thinks of last night, the memories before the drugs kicked in. The game was depraved and twisted, but she didn't hurt anyone. She didn't kill anyone. She'd remember, right?

But then she thinks of that lumpy black bag being loaded into the car. What was that?

It couldn't have been a body. That's ridiculous.

But where was Tina?

No. No.

Debbie pushes her thoughts away.

She's just getting creeped out. Strange things happened last night. It was brutal, evil, savage. But she has to try and let it go. Svetlana was right about that.

The mansion retreats behind her, somewhere in the desert. She doesn't even know where. Just some creepy mansion in the middle of nowhere. A little slice of hell. A place she never wants to think about again.

As she gets closer to the city, Debbie's internet reception comes back.

She has 7,340 notifications. The most she's had for months!

She goes through them. The shot of her in the lobby of the mansion in her red Valentino-like gown has 13,400 likes! Her most popular picture for ages.

Debbie feels a swell of satisfaction. How did it take off that much?

It's a good shot, but most of her pictures, even her best ones, don't get more than four thousand likes, five tops.

It turns out another influencer, Jenna Ray, has shared Debbie's post. Jenna, who was posing from the deck of a yacht on the Amalfi coast just a few weeks ago. Jenna, who Debbie was sickeningly jealous of.

Jenna has shared Debbie's post to her stories with the caption, 'Check out this BABE!' Jenna has a million followers. And now a bunch of them are paying attention to Debbie. They're following her. Her follower count has jumped by thousands.

Debbie smiles to herself. She knew this trip would pay off.

She sends Jenna a DM.

Thank you so much for sharing my post, hon! I so appreciate it!

She adds five love heart emojis.

Then she checks her DMs. There are the usual messages from sleazy men, hitting on her as though they're the first guy to have ever slid into her DMs. Debbie scans each message for a microsecond before muting. But there are a few messages, hidden among the junk, from brands. One from a travel company that wants to work with her. Another from an overseas beauty company. They're offering brand deals for twice the amount Debbie usually gets paid.

Excitedly, Debbie clicks onto her own page. She tries to see herself like a stranger would see her. All the shots of her posing at the hotel are undoubtedly impressive. She looks rich and successful. Bougie and aspirational. And gorgeous. Debbie can see why people would want her to represent their brands. She's objectively a very attractive woman, with her thick, long blonde hair, bright blue eyes, and slim, perfect figure. She's classically gorgeous, and she's glad she's finally getting some more attention. Some traction. She's been plugging at her Instagram page for a long time now and things have felt slow and static. It's about time her efforts paid off.

Debbie responds to the brands, telling them how much she'd love to work with them.

And by the time her driver reaches the hotel, she almost feels normal.

Until the wounds on her back sting as she gets out of the car and the panic lurking inside her rises a little.

Her driver doesn't offer to take her bags from the boot. There's an awkward moment as Debbie stands by the boot, waiting for him to get out and help, and he doesn't.

Debbie looks to the hotel. Is a concierge going to help?

A few stand by the entrance, looking right at her. But neither moves a muscle.

Debbie's surprised.

The staff were falling over themselves to help her before. They were bowing at her for goodness sake! And now they're acting like she's not even here.

'Could you open the boot please?' Debbie asks her driver.

He eyes her coolly and presses a button on his dashboard.

'It's open,' he says, sneering.

'Thanks!' Debbie replies sarcastically.

She gets her bags and heads into the hotel.

The concierges by the door stand, staring resolutely ahead like soldiers in front of the House of Parliament. It's like she's not even there.

Do they know what she did last night? Debbie wonders. Do the staff here know what girls like her get up to in that mansion? The degrading stuff they're paid to do? Is it a known thing at the hotel that Yusef invites desperate influencers to his desert mansion and entices them to take part in awful acts?

Probably, Debbie reasons, as she pulls her bags into the hotel. She thinks of the concierge who gave her the invite, with his courtly manner and his overly gelled hair. Did he know? And yet he was so obsequious. So polite.

Debbie doesn't want to think about it. It's too creepy. Too dark.

She just wants to get to her hotel room.

She walks over to the lift, heads inside and shoots up the shaft, and within moments, she's swiping her pass against her room door.

Inside, she breathes a sigh of relief.

Solitude.

Amelia's gone. Her bed's perfectly made, her stuff nowhere to be seen. Hardly a surprise. She's probably already descending onto English soil.

Debbie checks her back in the mirror.

There's blood on her tracksuit top.

So much for the tissue Debbie used to try to stop her back from bleeding.

Debbie takes off her tracksuit top.

It's worse underneath.

Her vest top and the tissues are crimson. Soaked right though.

'Fuck,' Debbie spits.

She takes her vest top off and puts it, along with her tracksuit top, in the bin.

She goes to the bathroom and peels the bloody tissue from her back. She puts fresh tissue on her wounds, but it gets soaked through. They're just too deep. When will they stop bleeding?

Debbie's phone buzzes. Jenna has replied.

You're welcome, babe! So glad you're having a good time.

More love heart emojis.

Debbie can't deal with this right now.

She can't do it, the Instagram fakery. Not now.

She puts her phone down and tries to halt the bleeding.

Eventually, with tissue stuck to her back and the bleeding abating ever so slightly, Debbie heads back to her bedroom. She catches sight of herself in the mirror. She's pale, ghostly.

She sinks onto the bed. She thinks about what she'd be doing right now if Amelia were here. Their itinerary. Maybe they'd be sightseeing. Or just lounging by the pool. So much for that.

Debbie reaches for the remote and turns on the TV.

She hasn't posted on Instagram since last night. Her followers, the keenest among them, will probably be wondering what she's doing, where she's gone, but she doesn't care. The last thing she wants is to go out sight-seeing, like everything's normal.

Her stomach squirms with anxiety and panic, and nothing feels okay.

Debbie wonders whether eating will help.

She orders a club sandwich from room service and then sits on her hotel bed, eating the sandwich and watching The Big Bang Theory on cable. She drinks a Diet Coke from the mini bar, pops some codeine she packed for emergencies, and tries not to think.

An email comes through on Debbie's phone. She sees it's from Samara, Yusef's assistant, and her stomach lurches. What does Samara want? Debbie doesn't want to have to deal with anything related to Yusef ever again.

Debbie opens the email. Samara is alerting her to the fact that a photo is missing from the content obligations of her contract. She's shared pictures on Instagram of everything on the list, except a photo in front of the hotel.

Debbie re-reads the email, thrown by its ordinary, business-like tone. Clearly Samara doesn't have a clue what happens to influencers at this hotel and why Yusef really invited her here.

Debbie takes a bite of her sandwich and tries to focus on the TV, as though to claim back reality even though it feels like it's blurring and she's disassociating.

She doesn't know what to do.

It's almost like she imagined last night. Like it didn't even happen. Like it was some warped figment of her imagination.

And yet, her bank balance would suggest otherwise.

Debbie googles Samara. A LinkedIn page comes up.

She looks a few years older than Debbie, maybe late twenties. She looks nice, put together, happy.

Debbie half wants to tell her about last night. Let her know what kind of people she's working for and what's going on.

But what can she say? Technically, the game was optional. She could have left like Amelia did. She did consent, in a weird way. She was paid. And if she says anything, it will get back to Yusef, and then what? Will she be told she's lying?

If she admits to engaging in sex work, then she's

breaking the law in this country. She could get thrown into jail. And that would be no picnic.

Debbie's palms sweat. She realises she's gagged.

She thinks of that NDA she signed, which she barely gave any thought to. She googles defamation laws here. It's a criminal offence, not even civil. A young woman was thrown into jail just two months ago for insulting her uncle on WhatsApp.

For insulting her uncle. On WhatsApp. What the fuck?

Debbie's head spins.

She's completely and utterly gagged.

Yusef has deeper pockets than she can even imagine. If she speaks one word against him, he'll come after her. No wonder she hadn't heard what really happens at this place. How many other influencers have been embroiled in dark activities here, only to realise afterwards that they can't say a word?

Debbie thinks of the chilling Google review she read before her trip, warning her not to come here. It was clearly left by another victim, who risked a lot by posting it. Debbie should have listened. She wonders what that girl's doing now, if she's safe.

Debbie clicks back onto Samara's LinkedIn profile. She probably doesn't have a clue what happens in this place. She probably thinks she has a nice job at a nice hotel working for a nice man.

Debbie feels an uncomfortable gulf between her and Samara. As though Samara is valued, protected, respected, and she is dirty, despicable trash. Would Yusef ever dare drive Samara to a mansion in the middle of nowhere and invite her to take part in sinister games? Doubtful. But why Debbie? What is it about her that made her seem like an appropriate person to do that to? And worse, why did she prove him right?

Sighing, Debbie checks the photos on her phone.

Surely, she took one in front of the hotel.

She and Amelia took hundreds of pictures when they got here. Thousands, even.

Debbie scrolls through her gallery, scrolls and scrolls, and double-checks, but there's nothing. Not a single shot in front of the hotel. Not even a selfie.

Somehow, when taking all the photos Debbie thought she needed, she forgot about the front of this place. For God's sake.

Debbie double-checks her contract, making sure Samara isn't mistaken, and yet there it is: 'A photo of you in front of the hotel featuring signage, with the hotel tagged.'

Great.

The last thing Debbie feels like doing is getting made up and going and posing in front of this hell site. But she has to. She signed a contract stating she would.

She doesn't want to get on the wrong side of Yusef. She just wants to lay low until she can leave here and get as far away as possible.

So Debbie finishes her club sandwich and starts looking for something to wear.

Demure this time, she goes for jeans and a nice blouse, big Chanel sunglasses—at least they'll give her some privacy.

She styles her hair and does her face, applying heavy foundation, contouring, blusher.

She has eye bags and her face is puffy. She's not exactly her best self, but the makeup hides it to a degree. And it's not like this picture is going to be a close up. She'll get someone else to take it.

Inspecting her reflection in the mirror, satisfied, she heads downstairs.

She's in a daze from the codeine, which takes the edge off the experience of asking a stranger to take her picture and smiling and posing in front of the hotel. In front of this grotesque fucking place.

Back in her hotel room, Debbie inspects the photos. They're surprisingly good, considering how she feels. You'd never be able to tell she'd been lashed with a horse whip the night before.

They don't capture her sweaty palms, her racing heart, her complete disorientation.

Debbie chooses her favourite, does a few tweaks, and then thinks, 'Fuck it,' and posts it on her page.

She adds a generic caption, hating herself with every word: 'Had a great stay at Mirage Royale!' She adds some smiling emojis, a sun one, and tags the hotel.

She sends Samara an email, confirming that she's posted the picture.

It already has 130 likes.

And they keep coming.

Along with the comments.

'Looks like you're having such a good time, hun!'
'Wow, that place looks INCREDIBLE'
'Looking beautiful as ever, queen!'

'Have a blast, Debbie!'

Not bad, Debbie thinks as the likes and comments pour in. The Mirage Royale Instagram account shares her picture to their stories, thanking her, which makes the post fly even more. Debbie wonders if Yusef did that and she feels weirdly dizzy at the prospect.

She gets up off the bed and paces the room. The movement causes the wounds on her back to bleed.

She looks down at the bed and sees she's left patterns of blood on the white sheets. A surreal, bloody crisscross.

CHAPTER THIRTY

Debbie wakes up after having slept for just two hours.

She tries to get back to sleep. She's flying back today. She doesn't need to be up for a while, but she feels uneasy.

Her wounds sting and throb, and she can't get rid of a shaky feeling in her chest.

Debbie wonders if she'll be able to sleep back home. What if this restlessness is her new normal now? What if anxiety never leaves her? What if she'll never be able to feel settled and peaceful again?

Reflexively, Debbie grabs her phone and checks Instagram.

Yusef has liked her latest picture from his personal account. The shot of her smiling outside the hotel.

Debbie feels sick. He's liked her picture, like nothing happened. She wants to scream.

He no doubt gets off on the idea of her standing outside the hotel, smiling for the camera, knowing inside that she's crumbling. He knows that behind that smile and under her clothes, she's wounded. Literally and emotionally.

Debbie clicks onto his page—all slick pictures of sports cars and holidays with his glamorous smiling wife.

Debbie clicks onto the 'block' button and then hesitates. She can't quite bring herself to do it.

What if he notices and gets offended? What if he retaliates in some way? What if somehow he gets the money out of her bank account? She wouldn't put it past him to have a contact in banking who could do that.

What if he has footage from the other night and leaks it? There could have been hidden cameras. Debbie wouldn't put anything past him and his sick friends.

Debbie hates herself for it, but she's scared; she's rattled. She's deeply uneasy.

She has a WhatsApp message from her mother.

'Hope you're having a good trip. Angel had a pasta dinner.'

The message is accompanied by a picture of Angel, sitting cutely on her mother's kitchen floor, next to a near-empty bowl of pasta.

Something about the picture, the message, and the uncharacteristic niceness of her mother makes Debbie cry.

She cries into her pillow, silently, and she lies there until the sun comes up and her alarm goes off.

CHAPTER THIRTY-ONE

Packed and ready to leave, Debbie wheels her suitcase down the corridor from her room towards the lifts.

None of the hotel staff rush to help her with her luggage anymore. They were falling over themselves to please her and Amelia when they first arrived, opening doors, carrying bags, showing them around, bowing to them as though they warranted deep respect. They were treated like royalty.

Was that all part of the grooming process? Build them up, make them think they're special, just to knock them down, show them where they really stand?

Debbie wonders whether all the staff know what happens at the mansion. If the English girls who come here are just a big joke.

She pushes the thought out of her mind and gets into the lift, pressing the button for the ground floor.

The doors close, and the lift travels down the shaft.

Three floors down, four. Each floor descended is a step closer to home.

Home.

Debbie has never wanted to go home more in her life. Each step, each floor, each moment brings her that little bit closer. She just has to keep going. Just keep going.

On floor 12, a woman gets into the lift with her partner.

A quick scan, head to toe, reveals that tens of thousands of pounds have been spent on their outfits. Hermès, Prada, Gucci, Balenciaga, a snakeskin Birkin that could probably cover Debbie's rent for years. Even more has been spent on the couple's jewellery: diamonds, rubies, and sapphire rings, Rolexes, and Cartier. The woman's perfect skin, unbelievably glossy mane, flawless skin smooth as silk, and emerald eyes, as well as her fragrant scent like an orchard in spring, make Debbie wonder if she's Arabian royalty perhaps. Or a famous actress. Someone of an entirely different league.

Debbie, who is used to being the prettiest or at least one of the prettiest in the room, suddenly feels ugly, misshapen and gross. Compared to this woman, she is a monster. She is the elephant man. She is a genetic abnormality, a runt. She looks away, averting her eyes, vaguely taking in the lift's polished wall.

She feels the woman looking at her and instinctively sucks in her stomach.

She feels cripplingly self-conscious about the dupe Gucci trainers she's wearing, her non-designer luggage, the bruising on her neck, and the spot emerging on her chin.

Her palms start to sweat. The woman is still looking. Debbie can't help glancing her way. Their eyes meet. The woman's beautiful green eyes laser into hers. Her husband also stares.

Debbie smiles awkwardly. The woman smirks.

Debbie's chest tightens. The woman looks away.

The lift draws to a halt, its doors opening.

'Sharmouta,' the woman spits. Her partner laughs.

Debbie can't look at either of them.

She doesn't know what sharmouta means, but she knows it's not exactly good.

Eventually Debbie looks up as the lift doors close, but the woman and her partner haven't gone. They stand on the other side of the lift like demons, smirking and sneering.

The doors close.

Debbie's palms sweat. She's lightheaded with anxiety.

Why can't she be left in peace?

Why do people have to stare? Judge? Why can't they just leave her alone?

She wants to be in different skin. She wants to be a different person.

The lift doors open at the ground floor, and Debbie tries to hold it together.

She wants to cry. She wants to crumble. But she has to hold it together to cross reception. She has to hold it together to get home.

Debbie feels like everyone is looking at her as she emerges from the lift.

Looking at her and seeing she's a fraud, an interloper, a poor English nobody who thought she could live it up here in this wealthy city. A silly girl who mistakenly believed she was important, thought she was on the rise.

What a fucking loser. What a joke!

Debbie looks to the exit, the waiting taxis visible through the plate glass, and she charges across reception, her gaze fixed on escape.

'Miss? Miss?' Someone is saying.

Debbie ignores them. She *has* to get out.

'Miss?'

Debbie turns, red-faced, ready to cry or scream.

A woman in a hotel uniform, young, eighteen, nineteen perhaps, with wide, sweet-looking eyes, holds out her passport.

'Are you leaving? Your passport?'

In her desperation to leave, Debbie forgot to check out. She left her room spotless, with her room card inside, but completely forgot about getting her passport from reception.

Debbie takes her passport from the sweet-looking woman.

'Thank you,' Debbie gushes, fleetingly, horribly envisaging the prospect of having realised at airport check-in, having had to come back, having missed her flight. 'Thank you.'

'You're welcome.' The woman smiles and heads back to reception.

Debbie places her passport in her bag, zipping it safely into a side pocket, and then she steps out onto the street and puts her sunglasses on. The light feels particularly bright on so little sleep. Everything's hazy, hallucinatory, oddly fragmented.

Debbie approaches a cab.

The driver agrees to take her to the airport but yet again, doesn't offer to help with her bags.

Debbie loads them into the boot.

As the car leaves the hotel, Debbie googles 'sharmouta'.

'Sharmouta is a highly offensive Egyptian expression that means whore or a prostitute', Google tells her.

Debbie wonders if the woman in the lift knew the kinds of things she'd been doing, that she'd been on the floor, whipped, abused, spat on. That she'd eaten dog food, and all the other despicable deeds.

Does everyone around her know? Is it just a running joke that desperate English girls let themselves be abused for money?

Or perhaps she just looks like an everyday prostitute.

The streets beyond the car window are teeming with tourists posing for pictures. Frenetic and fast and full-on in a way that Debbie cannot tolerate.

She closes her eyes. Blots it out.

She's here but not here.

She checks out, shuts down.

For the next few hours, Debbie stays on autopilot, going through the motions at the airport, zombie-like, until her body and mind finally grant her relief on the plane home to London, and she falls asleep in seat 11E under a complementary blanket, soaring above the Atlantic.

CHAPTER THIRTY-TWO

When Debbie gets home, the trauma and exhaustion hit.

The wounds on her back become infected and throb with pain. Pain she cannot ignore.

Feverish and delirious, writhing in bed, Debbie calls her mother.

Gillian comes to her flat, sees Debbie, white as a sheet, Angel whining by her bedside, and she calls 999.

At the hospital, Debbie is treated for potential sepsis. She stays there a week.

Debbie is asked by caring nurses and even a police officer, who has been hurting her, but Debbie trembles. She thinks of those men, with their money and their power and their influence. Their dark eyes. She thinks of that room and all the horrific, grotesque things that went on in there. She thinks of the things she did. The things she can remember and the things she can't. She doesn't want an investigation, if that were even possible. She doesn't want to know. She thinks of the NDA she signed with Yusef. She thinks of the penalties for slander in that country, the possible consequences of speaking out.

She thinks of the laws banning sex work, the legal penalties of her transgressions. Could she get penalised, even though she's on home turf now? She doesn't know, and she's not going to risk it.

So she stays quiet.

And the officers and the nurses sigh and shake their heads.

They try to get her to speak, but she won't let up. She won't even speak to her mum, and the whole incident becomes yet another thing between them that they leave unsaid.

The officers resign themselves to Debbie being yet another victim, protecting the person damaging her the most.

CHAPTER THIRTY-THREE

Later, Debbie buys a flat.

She uses the money she earned that night. She wants something solid. She still worries the money could be taken from her bank account. Somehow. Someone with power and connections could take it. She doesn't know exactly how, but the fear is there. If the money is in a house, it feels harder to take.

Debbie searches for flats across Essex, not telling anyone. No one knows about the money. How could she explain it? It doesn't make sense to go from a broke influencer to a homeowner pretty much overnight.

Debbie views half a dozen places, trying to find the right one. The house hunt gives her something to focus on, something to think about that isn't that night, something to latch onto to feel just about normal.

One day, she views a flat in Chigwell and stops in at a café around the corner.

Sipping a cappuccino and scrolling, Debbie feels someone looking her way. She looks up to see Amelia and Sam, clearly together now, standing in the doorway.

Amelia looks stunning, glowing. Her hair is shinier and glossier than ever, and she's dressed down, in Uggs and leggings, but with her unmistakable Balmain leather jacket, she looks somehow incredibly dressy. And yet Debbie takes in her shocked gaze, the look of disgust, alarm, and pity in her eyes.

A beat passes in which both girls just look at each other.

And then Amelia says something quietly to Sam, and they turn and leave.

Debbie feels small, embarrassed.

She's a person to be shunned, avoided.

She imagines what Amelia might be saying to Sam about her as they walk away down the Chigwell street. She doesn't want to think about it.

She quite liked that flat. It was nice, spacious, and modern, but she knows she won't be putting in an offer now. She doesn't want to risk running into Amelia again.

She doesn't want to have to feel so small again. So shameful.

So she keeps looking. She tries to tell herself that at least she has money. At least she has some security now. But no matter how hard Debbie tries to put a positive spin on things, she still lies awake most nights, unable to sleep, haunted by what happened in that mansion. There are things she can't remember. Great big chasms. Everything after Lydia quit the game is still a blank. Debbie knows bad things happened after that point; her bank balance would testify to it, but she doesn't know what. She doesn't want to know, but not knowing is also terrifying. She thinks of the feeling she got when she was with Stephen. A dark, detached feeling, and it makes her palms sweat. Where did she go that night? Where did her morality go?

Some days, she tries to put the night out of her mind. But there are always reminders. Reminders that leave her stunned and reeling. One of the estate agents has a laugh like Nigel's, and Debbie practically bolts from the property. She can barely even bring herself to respond to his emails.

She pops out to buy some milk one day when, in the queue at the corner shop, she stands behind a man wearing aftershave she vaguely recognises from one of the men that night, and her chest tightens, her palms sweat, and her breathing is choked for the rest of the day.

Debbie wonders if she's always going to be like this. Triggered. On edge. If this is her life now.

Eventually she finds a flat, completing a quick cash sale. She settles into the nice one-bedroom apartment in a development full of young professionals, upstanding PAYE people, with mortgages and hatchbacks and pension plans, and she feels strange and seedy, an interloper. And yet the flat is hers. She's earned it, in her own way. She doesn't have to answer to anyone.

She's not exactly proud, but she's glad to have the place. Brick walls. A base. A home no one can take away.

Debbie told her mum she was moving house but pretended she was still renting. It's a relief not to have to go to her mum anymore on quiet months, asking for money to pay the rent. She never wants to have to do that again.

The financial freedom is a deep relief. Debbie feels less fraught, less desperate. She doesn't have to sell gifted clothes and beauty products on eBay to make ends meet. She doesn't have to work with rubbish brands as much, flogging products for whoever will pay like a QVC saleswoman.

The security of her flat gives her a bit more peace. It allows her to be selective.

She gets a few respectable brand deals. It's regular work and enough to pay the bills.

Which is good, because there are days when Debbie can barely get out of bed.

She finds she's not leaving her flat for days on end. She can't bring herself to. It simply feels like too much effort. So she draws the curtains and retreats. She gets weekly food deliveries from Tesco. She hires a dog walker for Angel, who picks her up every day, while Debbie in the dark and goes over that night. It replays in her brain. It won't stop replaying.

Debbie looks up the other girls online, the few whose handles she managed to get.

Svetlana is acting like nothing happened. Her feed is as lively and flawless now as it was before. There's nothing that would indicate that she was ever beaten and abused on a mansion floor halfway around the world.

Tina's profile is still there, but she hasn't posted since that trip. Her last photo is a shot of her smiling on a lounger at Mirage Royale. Did she quit

Instagram? She must have found the whole thing too much. Or at least that's what Debbie tells herself. She refuses to contemplate a worse reality. Doing so would open a door to darkness she may not come out of. She thinks of what Svetlana said. *What happens in the mansion stays in the mansion.* In a way, it was good advice. Because if Debbie allows herself to question what happened that night too much, she isn't sure she can take it. She blocks Tina and forces her out of her mind.

Lydia seems to have disappeared. Her profile picture has been replaced by nothing but black, and all but one of her posts have been deleted. The only one remaining is a video of a hike she took three years ago, to the top of the Malvern Hills, with her kids. Something about that black chasm of a profile picture gives Debbie chills. She sends Lydia a message, checking to see if she's okay, if she wants to talk, but she gets blocked. At least she knows Lydia's alive.

Debbie orders a ton of fruit and spends two days making content featuring the juicer she's still being paid to promote. She puts on different outfits and films at different times of day. She invents contexts and makes quirky comments and cute jokes. She makes it look like her posts are being made in real time over the course of a couple of months, and then she saves them all to a file on her phone to drip-feed out, and she goes back to bed.

Debbie reads.

She reads books she'd gathered over the years. A few romance novels were sent to her years ago by authors and PRs in the hope she might post something about them on her page. She never did. Romance novels weren't her thing then, and they're not now.

She needs darkness. She reads a few thrillers, which almost hit the spot.

And then she starts ordering books online.

She orders books on psychopaths. Dark triad personalities. Sadists. She educates herself on all kinds of personality disorders. Some of the information is helpful. And some of it doesn't quite convince her.

The consensus is that psychopaths don't feel empathy, but Debbie isn't sure she believes this. She's never met anyone who doesn't have any empathy, absolutely none at all. She's never met a person who is one hundred percent bad. Her dad dropped her like she was nothing, but she still has memories of how he used to stroke her hair and let her snooze on his lap, watching TV when she couldn't sleep. He physically couldn't walk past a homeless person without giving them something. He used to fundraise, doing marathons for the local animal shelter. He wasn't all bad, as much as Debbie sometimes wishes he was. If he'd been all bad, then she'd have been able to hate him more easily. She'd have been able to let go.

No. The men she met that night are probably considered reasonable people, good dads, or decent husbands back home. They probably have causes they support. Moral Achilles' heels. Perhaps a lot of their decency is an act, but Debbie doubts they're bad every second of the day.

They were capable of disgusting, evil acts, but they probably had some empathy for their kids or their dog, perhaps. Their brand of empathy is just more selective than most people's. They can turn it on and off. Compartmentalise it. And they don't care that that makes them hypocrites. They don't care at all.

The psychology books seem to want to put people in boxes: psychopaths, sociopaths, narcissists, etcetera. Us vs. them. But Debbie isn't convinced people can be categorised quite so neatly. Her biggest fear is that there is evil in all of us. A potential for darkness. And that with the right amount of power or money or corruption, 'normal' people could also do awful things. People like her.

Debbie abandons the psychology books. She's not interested in deluding herself, trying to impose order on chaos.

She starts reading theological texts. What fascinates her now is how people find meaning in this jarring, terrifying world.

She starts with *The Bible*. Moves onto *The Koran*, *The Talmud*, *The Teachings of Buddha*, *The Tibetan Book of the Dead*.

She drinks coffee and reads. Eats and reads. Goes on her treadmill and reads. She starts walking Angel again and comes home and reads.

She reads and reads.

Books are more interesting to her than the people she used to spend time with. She has no desire to go out. Her life no longer makes any sense, and she can't put on an act like she's still a regular girl.

She worries people she knows have heard things from Amelia. She doesn't want to have to lie about her life and how she got her flat. She doesn't want to pretend to be normal and just like before when she's simply not.

But she keeps up appearances online. Just about.

She keeps her Instagram account going.

She goes out for two days a month with a photographer and takes pictures at around ten locations a day: cafes, shopping centres, gardens. She changes her outfit for each picture. Every outfit is perfectly planned and packaged in a zip bag.

Then she drips out the content over the course of the month with captions that give the impression it's happening in real time.

Debbie knows she's changed. She knows her behaviour isn't normal.

There was Debbie from before that night, and now there's Debbie after. And sometimes she just stares into space and thinks about that.

The night in that mansion ripped her open, tore her apart, took all her foundations—her sense of self, safety, and security in the world—and left her a trembling mess on the floor. She's never felt such heightened fear, such pure adrenaline.

And now, all the things she used to care about—the number of likes on a post, how popular she seems, how slim her thighs are—feel stupid, irrelevant, utterly petty. They don't even register in her consciousness anymore.

Nothing rattles her. Nothing touches the sides.

Nothing makes her laugh anymore either. Sometimes Debbie thinks back to the laughing fit she had with Amelia on the plane in first class, and she feels loss. A cutting loss. Because that kind of thing doesn't happen now.

Debbie is reminded of a phrase on a fridge magnet belonging to one of her university friends back in halls: 'Man's mind, stretched to a new idea, never goes back to its original dimensions'.

Debbie feels like her mind will never go back to its original dimensions.

That night split her heart and soul open, traumatised her, and yet she's emerged weirdly different. Reborn. A darker, calmer Debbie has taken the place of the one before.

Life used to be a rollercoaster of ups and downs, and now she is unmovable, unshakeable.

When you've been lying on plastic sheeting, getting brutally whipped, when you've been cut and abused, humiliated and laughed at, when you've fearing for your life, and you've survived, none of the little things matter much anymore.

Sometimes Debbie thinks about her past. About leaving university and how much she beat herself up over it. And she realises, calmly and logically, that she could do something about that.

She doesn't have to give up on her old dream. The academic life. Books and cardigans and a cute, terraced house. She could still have that life. She's only twenty-five. Her life is not over.

So she looks into reapplying to university. She decides to study theology this time. It fascinates her in a way no other subject has.

She researches courses, writes a personal statement, and digs out her old exam certificates and wonders why this whole thing has taken her so long.

The old Debbie, on some level, likely feared getting rejected and feeling like even more of a failure. So she stayed in her cocoon. She carried on scrolling and pouting and posing and pretending everything was okay.

But Debbie's empty now, and she doesn't care. If she fails, she fails. If she doesn't, then great.

She sends applications off. Trying to spin five years as an influencer as a productive, valuable, and relevant endeavour is a bit of a struggle, but she just about manages it.

She ends up with two offers. One from a London university and one from Sussex.

She decides to go with Sussex and rents a little flat by the sea. She takes Angel with her.

It's strange at first, when the course starts. Debbie feels like an alien. She's been living online, scrolling, staring at screens for so long that she's almost forgotten how to be around people. Everything is very full on. Meeting people who don't have bios you can scan. Having interactions face-to-face multiple times every day. Smelling people's smell. Looking into their eyes.

It's a lot, and it takes Debbie a few months to adjust, but then she gets into it. She starts enjoying her life. She doesn't bother with any of the clubbing and craziness her cohort's getting up to. She's friendly with a few of the other students, but her favourite thing to do is study in her flat, at her desk in the bay window, the sea shimmering in the distance. She walks Angel on the beach every day.

In her second term, she takes a module on philosophical theology. Her lecturer, Ivan, is young, a PhD student. She notices his animated eyes and strong jawline, and the way he looks at her, paying attention, not just looking through or past her like most of the other tutors.

He's cute and a little eccentric, with longish, curly hair. He wears tweed suis like he belongs in another era. But he has a sweet personality and a sharp mind.

And one day, Debbie runs into him in town, and she asks him, directly, if he'd like to go for a drink. No fear. No shyness. No hesitation. And he says yes.

They go for drinks and dinner. They share stories about their lives and they meet up again the next day. They lie on the beach together and laugh and daydream and talk about hopes for the future.

Debbie feels her calcified heart softening a little, opening.

They get together and Ivan starts coming over to Debbie's little flat. He brings flowers, which wilt in vases on her windowsill, only to be replaced by fresh bouquets. They watch films, legs intertwined, and Debbie thinks of them in this little flat, its windows glowing with light under the Brighton night sky. She thinks of herself in a peaceful place, having found someone nice, and she can barely believe it.

Ivan lives in a wind-whipped terraced house with peeling paint near the seafront, full of books, with a cat called Hercules.

They go for walks on the beach, study in the library, and drink coffee in ramshackle cafes. Debbie plays with Ivan's cat, and they visit his mum in London, and life is normal, life is sweet, life is perfectly fine.

This is what she wanted. More than she wanted. More than she dared hope for. More than she probably deserves.

Ivan's supportive, nice. He respects her opinions and her dreams. He thinks her ideas for the PhD she wants to do have potential. He takes pictures of her for Instagram, the kind of content her followers love. Photos of her looking happy and cute, posing in The Lanes, eating ice cream on the pier, larky shots in the old arcade.

The likes are pouring in, and Debbie's follower count climbs even though she's not even trying that hard anymore. Brands reach out. And even Debbie's mum has started liking her posts.

Debbie just needs to stay calm, relaxed, and let this unfold. A life in which she's normal, valued, fulfilled.

One day Debbie wakes up and realises she's living her dream. She made it! She has a bookish, academic, contented life. She has what she wanted. And yet, and yet... There are days when she feels out of it, empty. Days when she shuts down and she feels like a ghost, an actor, a fraud. On such days, she flinches when Ivan touches her. She feels full of venom, and she needs to be alone. She avoids him, pretending she has deadlines, hoping he doesn't check her lies with the faculty.

On such days, Debbie wonders if she should break up with Ivan, let him find a girl who doesn't feel like a fake. A normal girl. A good girl. A nice person, the sort of person he deserves. But he says he loves her. He says he's happy. She can see it in his eyes. In his laughter and his smile and his affectionate touches. And she loves him too, she thinks, even though she feels sort of numb. So why take that from him? Why break up with him and hurt him?

Some days, Debbie still can't get out of bed. She pretends to be ill. As though battered down by endless colds and flus.

Sometimes it feels like there's a ball in her chest. A ball of something, she doesn't know what.

Just something in her chest: rage, anger, pain.

Something that makes her want to scream, shout, or punch a wall.

When she feels like that, she often gets drunk. Alone in her flat. Blackout drunk. Or she walks along Beachy Head, where the cliffs are eerily high, and if it's quiet, she screams into the wind.

Alcohol and heights, crashing waves, and fierce winds can make the feeling go away. For a while.

Debbie moves in with Ivan for her second year. She doesn't want to be alone. She's scared of herself.

She sleeps beside him at night. Feels him kissing her shoulder blades while she slumbers, where the scars have mostly faded now. Scars she's never explained to him and which he's never asked about.

He brings her breakfast in bed and buys her even more flowers, and they snuggle on the sofa bingeing series.

And yet the feeling, the ball of something in her chest, becomes more frequent. The darkness. The desire to do something... something bad. Something undefined. Something she doesn't understand.

She goes for a walk along the beach one afternoon, trying to get the winds to sweep away her darkness once more.

Ivan is at home, working on his thesis, making a casserole.

Angel runs across the beach, leaving soggy footprints in the sand. Cargo ships slide across the horizon, leaden grey against the sky.

The feeling won't go away.

And then a message request comes through on Instagram.

Debbie opens it.

Yusef.

Fucking Yusef...

Debbie's stomach flips, viscerally flips.

Hi Debbie,

I hope you're keeping well.

I'd like to request your presence at Mirage Royale. We're looking for guests for a private party. You will be handsomely remunerated.

Debbie laughs.

No way. Seriously, no way. She's about to block.

187

She thinks of the plastic sheeting. The tears. The fear. The panic. The lashings. The dog food. The blood. Every sick, twisted thing she did that night.

And then she thinks of the money, the freedom it's afforded her. The opportunities.

And she wonders what more money could do for her. Maybe she and Ivan could move into a nicer place, a bigger place.

On some level, she's dead inside. She died that night. She's different now. She knows that. Perhaps she could take more, earn more, use this emptiness. Use this screaming feeling, this aching ball in her chest.

Seagulls swoop overhead.

In the distance, the cargo ships slip out of view.

Debbie leans against a pillar underneath the pier.

She finds herself looking down at her phone.

She finds herself typing.

AUTHOR'S NOTE

Thanks for reading *All Expenses Paid*. I hope you enjoyed it, even though 'enjoy' may not be the right word.

As a writer, I'm drawn to dark subject matter. My debut thriller, *Pretty Evil*, was about a serial killer of bad men, and since then, I've been writing about troubling, traumatic themes.

I was inspired to write *All Expenses Paid* after hearing rumours circulating online about influencers being paid to take part in scandalous parties abroad, in which they were paid substantial sums of money by rich men to do degrading things. These rumours were gritty and underground, featuring mostly on Reddit and obscure YouTube channels, with unnamed perpetrators and victims, and yet something about them felt haunting to me, and I suspected there was no smoke without fire. I found myself wondering how such women got enticed to take part in such parties, what rewards they were offered, and how they felt afterwards. The allure of money is one thing, but how does a person cope spiritually after doing horrific deeds for cash? I felt drawn to writing about this topic but feared it was too out-there and potentially too crass.

Then it came to light that Hollywood elites have been engaging in sordid 'freak-offs.'. Suddenly, sinister sex parties and serious exploitation were not quite so underground, and I felt compelled to confront this topic.

I spent a lot of time imagining what kind of person would be drawn into taking part in such an event. No doubt a person who is damaged, like Debbie. The sad thing about exploitation and abuse is that damaged people are the easiest targets, and then they get damaged further. Debbie makes money, but she loses herself. And that is the biggest price to pay.

If you have enjoyed *All Expenses Paid*, it would mean a lot to me if you could review it on Amazon or Goodreads or spread the word on social media. I release novellas through my own imprint, Lighthouse Books, and as an independent author, I rely greatly on readers shouting about my books. Reader support truly means the world to me.

Thank you for reading, and if you'd like to connect with me online, I'm @zoerosiauthor on Instagram and my website is www.zoerosi.com.

If you enjoyed *All Expenses Paid*, you may also be interested my vigilante serial killer novel, *Pretty Evil*, available from Amazon, Waterstones and Barnes & Noble.

www.ingramcontent.com/pod-product-compliance
Lightning Source LLC
Chambersburg PA
CBHW022109170626
46808CB00002B/663